DO YOU HEAR WHAT I HEAR?

TULSA

ISBN: 978-1-957262-53-6 (Hardcover)
       978-1-957262-36-9 (Paperback)

Do You Hear What I Hear?

Yorkshire Publishing
1425 E 41st Pl
Tulsa, OK 74105
www.YorkshirePublishing.com
918.394.2665

Published in the USA

DO YOU HEAR WHAT I HEAR?

Helen Dunlap Newton

Dedicated to you, my son, Jonathan David. All your life, some of my favorite moments have been sharing a great book and hearing your thoughts. I thank God for your life and your courage.

Thank you to two special people who helped me understand the joys and struggles of experiencing cochlear implants. Arvel Eicher and Sandi Lawson, the insight you both gave me was valuable in making Noah's experiences believable. Thank you.

Thank you to my SCBWI-Oklahoma writing family. Your encouragement and critiques are always appreciated.

Finally, thank you for the support of my husband, my family, and friends. I am blessed to have each one of you in my life.

Chapter 1

Noah Baker had been awake for an hour.

Edgy, anxious. Waiting for light to peek around the edge of the blinds.

Waiting for his bed to vibrate and strobe light to pulse instead of an alarm he wouldn't hear.

Always waiting.

He glanced at his phone charging beside the strobe light. Wished there was someone he could text. Someone he could tell things he couldn't say to his parents. It had been a month since the surgeon inserted wires and stuff for the cochlear implant. Four weeks of waiting for the incision to heal and today's activation. At ten o'clock the technician would turn on the cochlear and Noah would know if he could hear.

Feel normal?

Maybe have hearing friends again?

He turned to his side and stared at a faint glow from the baseball resting on a holder on the wall shelf. The memory of his Little League team bringing the signed ball to him after their last game. The game he missed because of the accident. Noah pretended they would have won if he'd been there.

Not true.

He wasn't that good—as his brother reminded him every chance he got.

And then they moved away from everything familiar.

Mom said her boss transferred her, but Noah wondered if their move to Maryland was because of him. The extra bills and special doctors, because of him.

All Noah wanted was to be normal. Mom told him to be positive. Told him the cochlear would be a turning point in his life. Sometimes he wanted to yell at her to stop all the "life will be wonderful" talk. She didn't have to live the silence. But Noah didn't say the frustration out loud. It was better to stuff it down than see the pain in her eyes.

A year of silence and he was still lost inside his head. The memory of voices and sounds for company.

No baseball.

No friends.

Most kids don't line up to hang out with the new deaf kid.

Noah pulled the sheet over his head and tried to block out the panic that rarely left since that day his head hit the windshield. An urge to do pushups rushed through him. He needed to feel the burn in his arm muscles. To forget everything but breathing in and out. Ignore the future and concentrate on his pounding heart.

That wasn't going to happen either. The surgeon said no major physical stuff until this appointment.

Another hope for normal.

Noah's teeth rattled when his bed began to shake. He slammed the strobe light to stop the flashing and tremors. The idea of crashing the light against the wall was tempting but he stopped himself mid-throw. It wasn't like they could pick up another one at the local discount store.

More money.

From the side of his vision, Noah saw something come flying across the room. His brother's shoe bounced off his stomach and Noah fell back on his pillow. He leaned over the bed's edge and snatched the shoe from the floor. Then he pelted it back at Tod who had turned to face the wall.

He couldn't hear Tod's words, but knew they were there.

Angry words.

Always angry.

For the umpteenth time, he wondered why Tod was so mad. Shouldn't it be the other way around? Tod was the one driving when they slammed into the parked car. It was hard not to resent how his brother's mistake left him in silence and Tod without a scratch.

At least his brother hadn't aimed for his head. That would have been the target before the accident.

Before the surgery.

Everything was measured by before and after.

Before the accident, he and Tod had their own rooms. After the accident, and the move, they had to share. Tod hated it. Said it made him feel like a babysitter. Noah hated it even more. He longed for privacy. Ached for a place to escape Tod's constant put-downs. A place to think—to cry when he couldn't hold it back anymore.

Noah swung his legs over the side of the bed and touched the skin behind his left ear with guarded fingers. The surgeon said there would be dizziness after the surgery. Not much left now—except when he moved too fast. But what if this cochlear thing was bogus?

They made him read all kinds of freaky stuff about what could go wrong. Told him sounds wouldn't be the same as before. Told him he'd have to decide whether to do the second ear or not. If it didn't work would they take out the wires and leave him with a scar? That might be kinda cool. Maybe he could make up a tough sounding story of how he got it.

Girls dig scars, right?

Noah didn't want to think about it. Couldn't stop. He glanced at the jet models beside the baseball on the shelf. Pictured himself as the pilot in a cockpit until he remembered. They didn't let deaf people join the Air Force, let alone fly jets. He walked to the shelf and grabbed the models—glad he couldn't hear the crashing when he threw them in his closet. Sorry when Tod's second shoe reminded him his brother heard it loud and clear.

He shook his head to clear it. Regretted it immediately. His vision tilted and his stomach churned. He tried to relax with deep breaths in and out. Tried to center his vision. The spinning slowed and Noah caught a whiff of breakfast smells. He'd read that other senses got stronger when you lose one.

Noah took a deep pull of air and choked on the nasal burning stench from Tod's side of the room. Everything did seem to smell better or worse. Tod's fart bombs definitely fit the worse category. Noah threw his dirty socks at Tod's back, then headed toward bacon smells.

He searched his memory for morning sounds. Music blaring from the kitchen, squeaking shoes on the stairs, the sound of his own cough. But he was drowning in silence. Frustrated that all he had was the memory of normal, he slammed his hand on the stair banister then shuffled into the kitchen.

"Hey. Just in time," Dad's lips said.

Noah reached for a loaded plate. "Thanks." He felt vibrations in his throat. Wondered if his voice was nasally like a deaf kid he'd heard before the accident. Before someone pushed the mute button on his world.

"How come pancakes?" he asked. "Not Saturday."

Dad flipped the last one from the griddle to a plate and turned to face him. He pointed to his ear and said, "Celebration Day!" He raised a victory fist in the air then turned back to the griddle.

Noah knew he should be excited. Part of him was. Mom and Dad were like cheerleaders when they talked about the cochlear.

They were so positive everything would be perfect after activation. But the more they said it the more his panic spiraled.

No guarantees.

No guarantees.

No guarantees.

Dad slipped into a chair at the table and grinned. His teeth were bright against tanned skin. No history papers to grade since it was summer. Most mornings he'd be working his lawn business.

"Mom went to work early," Dad said, then raised a cup to his lips. "She'll meet us there."

Noah breathed in the coffee smell. Remembered Dad's hot liquid slurp.

Tod shouldered past him, making Noah's fork miss his mouth. Noah glared at him and signed a curse word. He wasn't that great at sign language, but he made sure he knew the curses.

"How come you're such a jerk?" Noah said. Surprised he'd said it out loud. At least he thought he'd said it out loud.

Even though it felt good to stand up to Tod, a part of him was sorry. Tod was the one person who didn't treat him like he was a freak or breakable. He liked that about his brother. Missed the fun they used to have playing whiffle ball in the backyard.

Noah watched Dad and Tod's lips move in what looked like an argument.

"Why?" Tod asked

"He's your brother!" Dad's face was getting red.

"Such a baby."

Noah almost laughed when Tod turned and signed his own curse word at him. He got it wrong, but Noah caught the meaning.

Tod grabbed a handful of bacon and stomped from the room.

Noah watched his dad massage his forehead. Wished he could tell him how nervous he was. How he didn't want to disappoint him and Mom.

Dad switched his frown to a forced smile when he saw Noah watching.

"Don't worry about your brother. We'll all be there with you today." Dad scooted his chair back, then pointed at his watch. "Finish up. Leaving in thirty."

Noah wished he could go to the appointment alone. Might be easier without everyone watching him.

Chapter 2

T he waiting room at Johns Hopkins was like a million other doctor's offices. Outdated magazines, toys for little kids, and the smell of new carpet.

Noah's eyes were closed, but he knew from her perfume when Mom slipped into the room. Still, he startled when she touched his hand. Her fingers were icy against his skin.

"You okay…?"

He'd been working on reading people's lips with his special ed teacher. He did pretty well with most people—except Mom. Her words were tough. Fast. Lips barely moving. It was worse when she was nervous. He guessed at what she said and nodded. She patted his knee.

For a second, Noah wanted to crawl onto her lap like he would have when he was little. She would kiss his head and say, *love you honey bunny.* His cheeks burned in embarrassment.

He glanced at Tod. Earphones on, eyes closed. Sitting as far away as possible. Noah missed music. Wondered what kind was playing through Tod's earphones. Jealous that Tod's ears worked.

The technician opened the side door and said something. Mom and Dad jumped up at the same time. Noah swallowed hard to keep his pancakes down and followed the family parade. Dad went back to get Tod.

Noah could feel his brother's eyes boring into his back.

The technician smiled and turned to face Noah when she talked so he could read her lips. He liked that about her. She led them into a room with chairs, speakers, and computers.

"Okay. Here we are. Noah, you can sit in the chair by the desk and your family can take the seats across from you."

Noah wiped his palms onto his jeans. It was like every test in school, every baseball game. He wished they'd flipped the sweaty palms switch in his brain while they were putting in the implant.

Stupid wish. The surgeon said they put the wires and stuff into the Mastoid bone behind his ear, not deep in his brain like he thought they would. He didn't even stay overnight in the hospital.

Mastoid was easy to remember because it sounded like mastodon. He used to have a poster of the extinct elephant on his bedroom wall. Not anymore. He put all the posters away.

Tod said dinosaurs were for babies.

Why did he let his brother get inside his head? Noah glanced in Tod's direction. Their eyes met for a brief second. Noah saw something he hadn't expected.

Fear?

That didn't make sense. His brother wasn't afraid of anything. Tod's life went back to normal after the accident. Not even a broken bone. Noah pushed away the resentment because it only made him more edgy.

The technician tapped Noah's arm. "I'm going to check the incision before we activate."

Noah nodded. He flinched when her gloved fingers touched the tender skin.

She leaned in front of his face and asked, "A little sensitive there?"

Again, he nodded.

She made the okay sign. "…won't interfere with…activation." He wished she didn't smell so good. Like some kind of flowers. It was hard to pay attention to the technical stuff her lips were explaining.

"Okay," she said, "let's get you activated."

Noah rubbed his palms across the legs of his jeans to dry the constant sweat. Panic rose in his throat as he watched the tech carry the processor from the counter to the desk. Her gloved fingers grasped the round part with one hand and the earpiece with the other. She scooted her rolling stool closer and lifted the processor to the side of Noah's head.

"Stop," Noah said. "I need a minute." He glanced at his parents and their worried expressions. His stomach turned when he saw Tod's eye roll. Knew what his brother was saying under his breath.

The tech set the processor on the table and touched Noah's arm. "It's okay," she said. "You let me know when you're ready."

He wasn't sure why he stopped her. He wanted it to work but if it didn't, it would be another failure. Personal. Like all the times he struck out and watched the disappointment creep across Dad's face.

But there was no going back now. He had to know one way or another.

He nodded and said, "Okay. Do it."

The tech smiled and picked up the processor once again.

Noah felt vibrations when it clicked behind his ear. He titled his head a little while she fastened the earpiece. He wanted to ask for a mirror. Would have if Tod hadn't been in the room.

The tech made some adjustments on the computer.

Noah could sense everyone in the room holding their breath. He waited. Closed his eyes and tried to remember how to listen. Noah startled with the first soft sounds he'd heard since the accident.

The tech faced him and said, "Tell me what you hear."

13

He struggled to separate words on her lips from the strange eeks and squeaks pouring into his brain from the cochlear. His heart pounded as sounds grew louder.

"Uh…it sounds like a robot. Even me." He thought he might be shouting. Everyone said the sounds wouldn't be the same as before, but this was like an electronic alien. He glanced at his family. Mom was crying and smiling at the same time.

He was shocked when the tech grinned. "That's good," she said. "I'll make a few adjustments." Her fingers flew across the computer keyboard. "Is that better?"

"No!" Noah shouted. Something had to be wrong with the implant. He sat on his hands to keep from ripping the magnet from his head.

"Noah. Noah!" The tech got in his face. "Look at me. This is normal. Don't panic."

Noah took deep breaths. Even that sounded like static and whistles.

She touched his temple and said, "It's going to take time for your brain to catch up." The technician held up one finger, rolled the stool across the room, and picked up the phone. Her words clicked and squealed through Noah's cochlear. She stood and turned back to him with a huge smile.

"Today's your lucky day, Noah Baker," her lips said.

Yeah, right. Noah thought.

"A doctor from the cochlear manufacturer is with us for a few days," the tech said. "He wants to talk to you. Is that okay?" She glanced at his mom and dad.

Dad shrugged and indicated it was up to him.

Noah blew out his breath. Couldn't stand the thought of another person being in the room.

"Do I really have a choice?"

"Of course," the tech said, "just let me…"

A tall man with grey hair and a goofy grin pushed through the door before the tech could finish. His cologne was strong and seemed to hang in the air.

"Noah, so nice to meet you." The man held out his hand to Noah and they shook. "I'm Dr. Ivan Odor."

Maybe Noah was distracted by the squeaks in his implant and hadn't read the doctor's lips. He glanced at the man's nametag. There it was, DR. IVAN ODOR. Noah covered his mouth with his fist. Coughed to disguise a laugh.

The doctor smiled and said, "Kind of a weird name, huh?" He pointed at his nametag. "Thought about having it changed, but if my father, Urah, can put up with it, I guess I can."

It took a second for everyone to put Urah with Odor. Laughter pushed tension out the door like an invisible hand.

Dr. Odor patted Noah's shoulder. "Okay, let's get to your implant. How's it going?"

Noah swallowed. "I can hear but it's all whistles, and weird sounds." Noah didn't look at his parents. Knew their foreheads would be wrinkled. Eyes worried.

"That's typical," Dr. Odor said while typing. "We can make things better with some adjustments but it won't sound normal to you for a while. How's that sound?"

It seemed different than it had in the beginning. Voices hissed like snakes saying words. He recognized some of what the doctor was saying, but it wasn't even close to normal.

He looked at mom's face. So hopeful.

He lied.

"Better. Much better."

Chapter 3

Pop! Hsss! Eeem...awk!

On the way home, Noah flinched through the odd sounds screaming in his head. Riding in a car had been scary since the accident. He managed to suffer through it when he couldn't hear the traffic. Now, the roar of the engine, traffic noises, even the turn signal was magnified into demented robotic sounds. He knew he should be grateful to hear anything but the alien invasion in his head was driving him crazy. He felt like a stretched rubber band, ready to snap.

Noah's fingers searched for the on/off button the tech showed him. Frustrated, he reached for the magnet and pried it from his head. The silence was instant relief.

He was glad Mom went back to work. Glad Tod was checked out with his music in the front seat—even though Noah wanted to rip the earphones from his brother's head.

Dad's eyes flicked from the road to the backseat.

"You okay?" his lips said into the mirror.

"Sure. Just needed a break."

Noah turned toward the window, so he wouldn't see Dad's eyes in the rearview mirror. Traffic slowed next to a water park where a kid flew down a steep slide and hit the water with a splash. Noah tried to remember what that much fun felt like. As the traffic sped up, a red truck blurred past them. Dad slammed on the brakes when it cut in front. Noah's mind raced backwards.

To Tod's words, "Unbuckle and get my phone."

To squealing tires, shattering glass and a white, hot thud.

To silence.

He needed the nightmare to stop. Needed either to throw up or hit something. He squeezed his eyes shut and punched Tod's seat.

Hours after the appointment, Dad left to mow a cemetery and Tod escaped to football practice. Noah, in his room, without an audience, grunted as he counted his twentieth pushup. His arms ached but it was a good hurt. Sounds were still weird, but he didn't feel as panicked. He stood and wiped sweat from his face with the bottom of his t-shirt. His hand grazed the cochlear and he remembered things the tech and the doctor said to do for practice.

He grabbed his phone from the bed and clicked on an audio book he'd downloaded for school before the accident. The tech said to listen to a story while reading the book. He rolled onto his bed to reach the bottom shelf of his bookcase. A baseball bookmark still held the last page he'd read. A tightening traveled up his back. He rolled his shoulders to loosen the tightness. Pressed play.

Seeing the words did help. Noah kind of recognized what he was hearing. The story drew him in until he remembered the settings the doctor said to try. He stopped the recording, then with cautious fingers, pried the round outside magnet from his head and slipped the processor from behind his ear. He pressed the button Dr. Odor showed him and returned the parts to his head.

"Hmm," he heard his robot words say. "That is better."

Excited, he switched from the audio book to his old music playlist. Smiled when the beat pounded inside his skull. When unrecognizable notes followed he yanked the processor from the back of his ear and fumbled for the button. There was another recessed dot next to it. He pressed both and slipped the processor into place. Nothing changed. Same hissing sounds posing as notes.

"Didn't press hard enough."

With the tip of a pencil, he pressed the extra button several times. When the music was still garbled, his disappointment threatened to suck him down again. He stuffed the phone in his pocket and went downstairs.

He'd guzzled half a can of Coke when Tod came through the back door with his football gear. A cloud of funky sweat walked with him.

"Burrrp!"

"Good one." Tod said. The hint of a smile soon switched to a scowl. "Better not be the last Coke," he threatened.

Noah leaned inside the fridge, then tossed a can of soda. Tod caught it and walked away.

Now you can throw? Too bad you couldn't do that in a game.

Noah choked on his drink when he thought he heard Tod's voice. "What'd you say?"

Tod turned back and hollered, "I didn't say anything, you weirdo!"

Noah heard scratch-squeak words, but it wasn't the same. He felt a kind of tingling.

Miss you, Noah. Miss the way things used to be.

"How can you miss me? I'm right here," Noah said.

Tod crushed the empty can and threw it at Noah. More scratchy words.

"…deaf! Now…crazy!"

Noah should have been mad, hurt by the insult he only half recognized. "Tod, Tod!" He ran toward his brother but stopped when he felt another head tingle.

Need a shower.

Noah grabbed the banister. Dropped on the bottom stair. Deep breaths.

Either the implant was really good or something was crazy wrong.

Noah waited for Tod to finish his shower and leave so he could be alone in their room. He intended to try the buttons on his cochlear but instead removed it and fell asleep on his bed. He knew Mom was home from work when he smelled her perfume and felt her cold hand on his cheek. He pretended he was still asleep rather than answer all the questions he knew would come. The truth was he was playing his conversation with Tod over and over. Maybe he wanted to hear real words so much he let his imagination take control. Did imagination get stronger like the smell thing did? When he couldn't stand wrestling with his thoughts any longer, he replaced the cochlear and went downstairs to face the parental third degree.

"Hey, sleepyhead," Mom said. "I thought you might sleep through supper."

He looks pale. Hope he doesn't have an infection. I should call the doctor.

There it was again. First scratchy robotic then a tingling and real words.

"No, Mom. I'm not sick. Just tired."

"Of course, you're not sick." Mom gave Dad a funny look. "I'm sure it's exhausting getting used to all the new sounds." She wiped her hands on a towel and kissed him on the forehead.

Well, at least his head is cool.

This time he knew she hadn't said anything, but he still heard her words. Noah studied a spot on the floor.

Struggled not to panic.

Knew he had to talk to Dr. Odor.

Chapter 4

Appointment number two, a day later. Same magazines, same smells.

Less family.

Noah felt a slight breeze as his dad fanned through a newspaper without reading.

Dad dropped the paper and touched Noah's bouncing leg. "Nervous?"

"A little," Noah said. "Just want it to be better."

Dad gave him a tight-lipped smile and a thumbs up.

That morning, Noah had waited to go downstairs until his mom left for work. He'd convinced his dad he was having bad pain from the implant. The audiologist clinic gave them an emergency appointment. Noah lied about the pain but didn't think he had a choice. No one would believe him if he told the truth.

"Noah Baker?" the robotic voice of a different tech called his name from the door leading to the exam rooms.

Noah stood too fast and felt everything tip. He grabbed his dad's arm and closed his eyes.

"You okay?" Dad asked.

Noah kept his eyes closed until the dizziness faded. He faced his dad and said, "I'm fine but I want to talk to Dr. Odor alone?"

"Not a good idea," Dad said.

Noah wiped his palms on the front of his jeans. "I need to take care of this myself."

Dad put his hands on his hips and stared across the room.

"Dad?"

"Okay. I'll wait here, but make sure you have them call me if you need anything."

Wow! Noah couldn't believe how easy that was. He hurried through the door before Dad changed his mind.

On the way to the exam room, Noah tapped the tech on the shoulder. "I need to talk to Dr. Odor. He said I should talk to him if I had any problems." Noah's heart was pounding so hard he had trouble getting out the words.

The tech's eyebrows scrunched together. "Sure, Noah." She pointed toward exam room number three. "Just have a seat and tell me about your pain first."

Noah faked his way through the pain questions before repeating, "I need to talk to Dr. Odor. Now!"

The tech's eyes went wide. She patted his arm and smiled. "Sure, I'll see if he's available."

Noah scrubbed his hands against his jeans and waited. He counted the number of tile squares on the floor. Felt guilty for lying and yelling at the tech. More scrubbing, more waiting. Finally, the door flew open and Dr. Odor filled the room. He held out his hand to shake while he read his computer pad. "So, you're having some pain?" He dropped onto a rolling stool and looked up.

Noah felt his face burn. "I lied. I knew you weren't going to be here much longer, and I was afraid they wouldn't give me an appointment. I'm sorry." He pulled in a breath and blew it out.

"Okay," said Dr. Odor. "Must be important or you wouldn't have done that. Tell me what's going on with your implant."

"There's something wrong with it," Noah whispered. "I'm hearing words,"

Dr. Odor smiled. "Noah, I think that's the idea."

"No," Noah said, "I'm hearing robotic sounds like before, but I heard my family say words." Noah leaned closer. "Dr. Odor, they *weren't* talking."

"Hmmm…" The doctor pressed his lips together. "Did you use any of the settings I showed you?"

Noah nodded and pulled the magnet from the side of his head. "I hope I didn't mess anything up, but I pushed this button too." Noah pointed to the tiny dot on the bottom of the processor.

Dr. Odor peered at the button, then rolled toward a round light on a stand. He slipped the processor underneath and turned it over and over. "Wait here."

"Oh, man," Noah groaned after Dr. Odor left. "Probably broke it."

More money.

More worry for Mom and Dad.

He slammed his fist against his thigh then stood and paced back and forth while he waited for the doctor to give him the bad news. He stopped to watch a tiny bird flitting in the tree outside the clinic window. Its yellow beak opened and shut every few seconds. Noah tried to remember the sound. What would a robotic chirp sound like? He wished Dr. Odor hadn't taken the cochlear processor with him.

Noah didn't see the door open behind him. Jumped when Dad touched his shoulder.

"Sorry, son." Dad's forehead furrowed deep and his eyes showed his concern. "The technician said Dr. Odor wanted to talk to us together."

"Don't worry, Dad. It's nothing." He felt a surge of regret for not telling his dad the truth.

The door opened, and Dr. Odor made the room seem smaller. He was trying to smile, but his eyes told the truth. Something was wrong.

Noah's stomach did a roller coaster flip.

Dr. Odor held out his hand to Noah's dad. They shook. It frustrated Noah that he couldn't read their lips. After a few minutes of Noah guessing what they were saying, the doctor turned and snapped the processor back into place.

"Noah, I don't want either of you to worry. We're just finding some unusual results with your implant. We'd like to run a few tests in the hospital."

Dad stood up. "The hospital? Is that why he's having the pain?"

Dr. Odor rubbed his chin and said, "That's what we want to find out, Mr. Baker. Noah is hearing some sounds we haven't anticipated. We'd like to do further studies. It would be extremely helpful in our research of how to improve the cochlear."

"I understand your research is important, but..."

Dr. Odor interrupted. "If you're concerned about the cost, there won't be any charges."

"Charges? Are you kidding me?" Dad stood and slammed his hand on the exam table. "I'm concerned for my son, not what it will cost!"

"It's okay, Dad." Noah touched his arm. "I'd like to help."

The truth was, Noah didn't think Dr. Odor was telling them everything. He was convinced when the doctor looked him straight in the eyes and a tingle stirred in his head.

Convince him, kid.

Noah's eyes went wide. Dr. Odor smiled at him.

He knows, Noah thought. He knows I can hear the words.

Knowing that should have scared Noah but part of him was excited. How cool would it be to hear people's thoughts?

"When would he need to go?" asked Dad.

"Today. I need to, uh, run the tests before I have to go back to our lab." He stood and handed Dad a clipboard. "I just need you to sign this. It gives us permission to run the tests. He will need to be there overnight."

Dad glanced at the paper, then looked at Noah. "I need to talk to my wife first." He pulled out his cell phone and walked to the far corner of the room."

Noah couldn't catch Dad's words but understood the nodding.

Dad punched the off button then said, "Okay, where do I sign?"

He didn't read the paper. Shouldn't he read the paper?

Dr. Odor turned to Noah and winked.

Weird.

The same strange feeling washed over him. Like it had with Tod. And his mom. He heard the doctor's unspoken words.

Good job. Need to call Captain Billings.

Captain? Like Army Captain?

Dr. Odor took the clipboard from Dad. "The front desk will give you instructions." He reached to shake Noah's hand and said, "I'll see you at the hospital."

And then he was gone.

Noah and his dad stood facing the door as it closed. Dad turned and said scratchy words, "Well, let's get you to the hospital." Then the unspoken words came, clear as could be.

Oh, son. What have your mom and I done? I was afraid this implant was a mistake.

"Don't worry, Dad. They're going to fix this." The words more confident than he felt.

Dad cocked his head to the side and frowned. "Of course, it'll be fine. Let's get those instructions."

His dad walked into the hall and Noah followed. They had to wait a few minutes at the front desk while papers with directions to the hospital and admit orders printed.

Noah's head was a storm of questions.

"I don't understand," Dad said to the clerk. "Why is Dr. Odor sending him to Walter Reed Hospital instead of Johns Hopkins?"

The clerk at the desk typed on her computer, eyes never leaving the screen.

Noah shifted from one foot to the other.

Finally, the lady sighed and stopped typing. She handed Dad a stack of papers. "These are the orders he gave me. You'll need to talk to him."

Dad ran his hand through his hair then leaned into the counter. "Okay. I'd like to talk to him."

"I'm sorry, but Dr. Odor has already left for the hospital." Her fingernails clicked on the computer. "I suggest you talk to him there."

"Let's go," Noah said. He forced a smile. Tried to calm Dad down before he started yelling at the lady.

"Okay," Dad said then took his arm and guided him out the door. "Let's do this."

Chapter 5

T he hospital was huge with a tower in front and a massive amount of lower story buildings surrounding it. A large fountain with flowers along wide sidewalks made Noah wish they could stop and walk—maybe throw pennies in the water. It was probably supposed to make people feel calm. It wasn't working for him. He had chewed his way through all the fingernails on his left hand and started on the right. He wasn't sure what made him more nervous; that something was weird with the cochlear or how long until his dad learned the truth that he wasn't really in pain. And what about the doctor's thoughts of a meeting with Captain Billings? It was all so crazy.

Dr. Odor's smile when he left them in the exam room should have calmed Noah.

It didn't.

Dad followed the signs in the shadow-filled parking garage until he found an empty spot. He methodically put the car in park, turned off the key, and stared straight ahead with his hands gripping the steering wheel.

Noah held his breath. Waited for the brain tingle and Dad's real word thoughts. Robotic hisses came instead.

"It makes no sense why we're at a military hospital." Dad turned and squeezed Noah's shoulder. "But let's go find out why you're hurting."

Noah didn't know if it was the smell of car fumes in the parking garage making him nauseous or the panic that was building in his body like a balloon close to bursting. He scrubbed his palms against his jeans and followed Dad into the building. Wondered if he should stop this now and tell Dad about the voices.

Knew he couldn't.

The buzzes and clicks through his cochlear magnified in the large lobby and ricocheted through Noah's head. A guard directed them to a metal detector line.

"Remove all metal from your pockets and place bags on the conveyor belt," another guard instructed.

Noah spotted a sign: NOTIFY OF ANY IMPLANTS OR REPLACEMENTS. He pointed to his cochlear.

The guard gave him a *thumbs up* and said, "You might hear a buzz, but it's fine."

Noah trailed his dad through the metal detector, then they were directed to a large desk.

"Papers, please," another uniformed guard said.

Noah watched the guard type something into his computer. Felt a tingle in his head and the guard's thoughts about a ballgame he was going to watch on TV.

Dad took the print-out and visitor badges from the guard's hand.

"Make sure you follow the instructions," the guard said and pointed to the elevators.

When the elevator doors closed in front of them, Noah blew out the breath he'd been holding. His dad glanced toward him.

"A little intense, huh?"

"Just a little!" Noah said and forced a smile. He glanced toward the ceiling. "Somebody's probably watching us right now."

Dad glanced at the paper and pushed one of the buttons.

"ACCESS TO THIS FLOOR DENIED!"

"Dad!" Noah shouted above the alarm and grabbed the paper. "It says, 7-B Red." He pushed the red button himself and the alarm stopped.

Noah saw his dad's frown. Lips pressed in a tight line. Knew he hated making mistakes.

They both grabbed the wall rails when the elevator quickly dropped down instead of up. It did a soft bounce when it stopped. The elevator doors opened. Dr. Odor stood facing them with his arms open wide. That goofy grin stretched across his face.

"Welcome! Glad you made it. Just follow me." He turned to lead them down the hall, but Dad grabbed the doctor's arm.

"Just a minute, Dr. Odor. What's going on here? We had to go through a metal detector for heaven's sake. Just what kind of tests are you planning to do?"

"I assure you, Mr. Baker, Noah will be in the best hands possible. The tests we need are only done in this hospital. I promise, it will be fine."

Noah shrugged when his dad looked at him.

"So," Dr. Odor said, "are we ready to proceed?"

Dad rubbed his forehead. "Okay, lead the way."

The air smelled of floor wax and rubbing alcohol. Nurses and doctors in military uniforms all stopped working to stare as the trio walked past them. Dr. Odor led them to another hall with guards.

Dad squeezed Noah's arm so tight he winced.

Noah glanced at his dad's face and saw the same fear he'd seen from Tod in the doctor's office. "You okay, Dad?"

"Sure." He let go of Noah's arm and patted him on the back. "You're going to do great."

Noah wasn't convinced. Especially when his dad's thoughts rushed at him.

This is crazy. Can we trust Dr. Odor? I should stop this right now!

Dr. Odor showed the guards his badge. Noah's and his dad's badges were checked, then they were sent to a private room halfway down the hall. All the other rooms looked deserted.

Weird.

Dad put his arm across the doorway to stop Noah, but Dr. Odor spoke before Dad could say anything. "Noah, there's a gown on the bed. We'll give you some privacy to get changed. Mr. Baker, we have some paperwork for you to complete. Please follow me."

Noah stood with his mouth open for several seconds.

Stared at the closed door.

Wondered why his dad hadn't questioned the doctor more. He undressed and put on the gown before someone opened the door.

Noah groaned when he realized he'd worn his Spiderman underwear that morning. "Sure not going commando!" he said, then held the back of the gown and plopped onto a metal chair beside the bed. A shiver raced through him.

Maybe it was from the cold chair.

Maybe it was fear of what was coming next.

Chapter 6

N oah startled when he *heard* a scratchy knock on the door. "Come in," his voice squeaked.

"Hey, Noah. I'm Lieutenant Green. I'll be your nurse while you're here."

Noah squirmed on the chair and said, "How come you aren't a doctor?"

"Less time in school. More time with cool kids like you! Now if you'll just hop onto my hot ride here, we'll get your tests started."

Noah dropped onto the seat of the wheelchair and turned to look at Lieutenant Green towering behind him. "So, do I have to salute you or something?"

"Oh, I think we can let that pass. You look a little young to be in the military. Besides, I should be saluting you. You seem dog-gone important to a lot of people here. Ready?"

Noah nodded and wondered what he meant. He started to ask, but Lieutenant Green pumped him with questions—what sports he liked, did he have a dog, a girlfriend. That last one made Noah release a huff. "There aren't a lot of girls looking for a deaf boyfriend."

That could change.

Noah startled and turned to look at Lieutenant Green. The words had been clear.

Real. Words.

Just like his family.

And Dr. Odor.

And the guard.

Lieutenant Green stopped at a room labeled, LAB.

After the second vial of blood was drawn by the lab technician, Noah asked, "What are you, a vampire or something?"

"Maybe. You don't mind if I have a little taste, do you?" The tech smiled and made a slurping sound. Then she filled three more vials. When she removed the rubber band thing from his arm, Lieutenant Green handed him a plastic cup with a lid.

"Okay, Noah. Fill 'er up."

"What's that got to do with my cochlear?"

"Oh, you don't think they can make your implant work better by checking your pee?"

"Uh, no."

In the restroom, Noah wondered if there were cameras like he thought there probably were on the elevator. It took him forever to "fill 'er up." Finally, he finished, left the cup on a shelf in the wall, and washed his hands.

Lieutenant Green smiled outside the door. "Good job! Hop on and let's get you to x-ray."

Noah held the back of his hospital gown and dropped into the seat. "Can I have x-rays with this?" He pointed to his cochlear.

"Probably not, but that's what the orders say, so that's where we're going."

They came to a long tunnel-like hallway. "Hold on to your skirt, kid. Let's see if we can stir up a breeze." The lieutenant ran as he pushed the wheelchair.

The air rushing past Noah's face swished and squealed. It was so much better than just feeling it like he had before his cochlear. His lips stretched across his teeth in a grin. He liked the idea of a new before and after.

Lieutenant Green skidded around a corner and almost crashed with another wheelchair rolling the opposite direction.

"Sorry, Mayfield," said Lieutenant Green. "On our way to x-ray."

Noah heard the scratchy conversation between the two adults, but his full attention was on the girl in the wheelchair beside him. With her brown skin and eyes no color he'd ever seen, Noah couldn't help but stare.

"Hi," he said.

"Hello," she replied, then blew a purple bubble and let it pop.

"I'm Noah," he said. Surprised he got the words out.

"Congratulations," the girl said with a flat voice. "Aren't we supposed to be in the lab?" she shot at the person behind her.

Noah caught the unspoken communication between the adults. Eye rolls saying the girl was difficult.

She turned toward the soldier behind her chair and a blanket slipped from her legs.

A soft gasp slipped from Noah's throat when he saw shiny metal with a shoe on an artificial leg.

"What are you staring at, you weirdo?" The girl pulled the blanket tight and pushed the wheels of the chair forward.

"Uh, nothing!" Noah shouted to her back. "I didn't see anything."

But he did see. A coldness ran through him.

"Let's go, kid," Lieutenant Green mumbled.

* * * * * *

It turned out he couldn't wear the cochlear during the x-ray. The silence after the tech removed it did give him time to think about the girl with the amazing eyes and missing leg. He wondered how she lost her leg. Puzzled why she was so angry at him because he saw it. Heat rushed up his neck and burned his cheeks.

He tried to forget about her, knowing he'd probably never see her again. But her face and her angry words kept flashing into his thoughts.

X-rays complete, the lieutenant made a gesture toward the wheelchair. "Let's head back to your room," he said.

"Sounds good to me," Noah said. "How come they're doing all these tests? They didn't do this much when I got my cochlear."

"Doc will have to answer that. I'm just your buff chauffer." Lieutenant Green flexed the muscle in his arm and laughed.

Just as they were passing the guard outside the hall of Noah's room, he heard robotic words behind him. Smelled grape gum. He turned and saw the girl from the hall. Considered apologizing for seeing her leg. Wished he could get close enough to read her thoughts.

"Bet you're hungry. Burger okay with you, kid?"

"Sounds awesome," Noah said, then watched the girl being pushed to the far end of his hall. Her scowl reminded him of Tod.

"Can I put on my clothes? This open-back thing is humiliating."

"Sorry, bro. Not until the doc says he's done."

"Hey," Noah said, "where's my dad?"

"Not sure," said the lieutenant. "I'll check on that while I put in your food order. Be right back." He clicked his heels and saluted.

Noah hopped on the bed and was searching for the TV remote when his dad peeked around the corner.

"Noah! Thought I'd never find you." Dad's forehead was wrinkled and sweaty, lips pressed tight.

"Just got back from a bunch of tests. Where were you?" Noah asked—surprised how much better he felt with his dad in the room.

Dad dropped onto the metal chair beside the bed. He wiped his forehead with his sleeve. "Dr. Odor took me to an office on another floor and had me sign all kinds of papers. He told me how to get back here, but I got lost." He turned his body to face Noah. "Is the pain better?"

"Oh, yeah. They just ran the tests to make sure everything is okay." Noah watched while his dad went to the sink to splash water on his face. Decided to tell him at least part of what was really happening with his cochlear.

"Dad…?"

A sharp knock sounded on the door before he could finish.

Chapter 7

"Once again, Mr. & Mrs. Baker," said Dr. Odor as he tried to deflect their questions, "I assure you Noah will be fine. We'll do some brain wave tests tonight while he sleeps. You won't be able to stay in the room with him."

Convenient.

Noah knew the doctor was keeping information from his parents and from him, but why? Noah bit his lip and wondered if that was legal. There had to be a law against using a kid for medical experiments.

His mom sat on the side of the bed and pushed Noah's hair back from his forehead. "Brain waves? That sounds serious." She took Noah's chin in her hand. "Are you sure you'll be alright without one of us staying?"

Noah looked at Dr. Odor and felt a tingle in his head.

Convince them.

Noah squirmed in his seat and stared at the doctor.

"Sweetie, did you hear me? One of us could stay in the lobby if that would make you feel better." His mother ran her hand through his hair again.

He jerked away from her. "I'm not a baby, Mom!" He knew he sounded hateful and felt more and more torn between his parents' feelings and the silent messages from the doctor.

"Dr. Odor said they are giving me something to knock me out. It's okay. No big deal."

"He's right," Dad said. "We'll get a good night's sleep ourselves and come first thing in the morning."

Mom stood. "Well, if you're sure. Is there anything we can bring you?"

Noah leaned in to whisper in his mom's ear. "Underwear."

"Oh, Noah, you're not wearing your old Spiderman pair, are you?"

"Mom!"

Dr. Odor grinned. "No need to be embarrassed. I have a pair of those myself."

Everyone laughed. A mental picture of Dr. Odor in the cartoon underwear with a goofy grin popped into his mind and wouldn't leave.

Mom leaned in to kiss the top of Noah's head and then his parents were gone. He regretted not asking them to stay as soon as the door shut.

The room was silent except for the robotic hum of the air conditioner hissing antiseptic air. Noah realized he hadn't been alone with the doctor since he'd shown him the button on his cochlear.

"You know about the real words, don't you?" Noah asked.

The doctor pulled a metal chair across the floor. The scraping sound screech-squeaked through Noah's cochlear.

"Yes, Noah," he said. "I think it's time you got some answers about what you're hearing." He rubbed his hand across his mouth and chin. "This is going to take a little time and what I'm going to tell you is top secret. You must promise me you'll not share this information with anyone. Even your parents."

Noah rubbed his sweaty palms across his hospital gown and turned to focus on a picture of the Pentagon on the wall.

The Pentagon?

Military Hospital?

Top secret?

Something was wrong with all of it. Noah reached to grab the back of his gown and run out the door. But curiosity won over panic. He needed to know why real words sounded in his head when people weren't talking. Plus, there was that "no pants" thing.

"Noah, did you hear me?"

Noah turned to face the doctor.

"I'm serious, Noah. I've got to be able to trust you. I think I can."

Noah drew in a deep breath. "You can. You can trust me."

"Good. A lot of what I'm going to tell you is complicated, so stop me any time you have questions." The doctor looked toward the ceiling, then stared deep into Noah's eyes.

"I know you and your parents couldn't understand why you are in a military hospital."

Noah nodded.

"My company produces cochlear implants for people like you, but we also conduct work for the government. For the last couple years, we've been developing experimental implants. They not only help people hear but are also capable of reading neurological electrical transmissions from another person."

"What does that mean—neurological transmissions?" Noah asked.

The doctor rubbed the back of his neck. "It's a mouth full, isn't it? We'll simplify it by calling it 'NT'. In simple terms..." He hesitated and stared over the top of his glasses. "It's hearing someone's thoughts. Mind reading."

"No way!" Noah waited for the doctor to start laughing—to finish the joke and then tell him the truth.

"Absolutely true. We have worked on this for some time, but we had our first success today." Again, Dr. Odor stared over the top of his glasses like he was waiting for Noah to figure out something that should be obvious.

"Well, that's good, but what does it have to do with...?" Noah felt his breath sucked from his lungs. The room began to spin.

"That's right, Noah. None of our experiments have been successful until you pressed that button."

"No. Way!" Noah stood and paced back and forth.

"Why would you implant a government experiment in...me!?" He stopped and threw his hands onto his head.

"I'm a kid!"

Dr. Odor stood and walked to the window. The scent of the doctor's cologne was so strong he could almost taste it.

"It was an accident. We were implanting one of our agents with a cochlear in the same hospital, at the same time as you." His shoes tapped on the floor as he turned and walked closer to Noah. "We're not sure how it happened, but you received the experimental implant. That marvelous brain of yours gave us our first success."

"So, is that why you checked my blood and stuff? To see why my brain works with it?"

Dr. Odor grinned and leaned close. "That's right."

"And then you'll take it out?" Noah asked. "You know, give me a regular implant."

Noah held his breath.

Waited for a *yes*.

"That's where we have a problem." The doctor sighed and looked toward the door. "Your brain is the only one that has received thoughts." He stood and crossed his arms. "We've got to figure out why."

"So, you want to use me in some kind of science experiment?"

"We want to study you, but much more than that."

Noah's mind raced to anticipate what the doctor was going to say.

Dr. Odor clicked his pen and sat in a facing chair. He leaned in resting his elbows on his knees "You are about to be offered a rare opportunity, young man."

Noah tried to imagine what the doctor might say but wasn't prepared for the robotic words that came through his cochlear.

"Noah, we want you to work for the government."

Chapter 8

T he doctor's retreating footsteps pinged through Noah's cochlear. Noah bit into his thumbnail. Kicked Dr. Odor's chair.

"Should have asked more questions," he said between clenched teeth. Thoughts of the girl he saw in the hospital flashed across his mind. "Wonder what she would have done."

Panic slammed at him like a kick in the gut. "This is crazy! Kids don't work for the government." He shot off the high bed. "I gotta get out of here."

Noah was stuffing his legs into his jeans when he heard footsteps returning. Too late. He threw his clothes in the cabinet and slipped into the bathroom—hoping to buy some time.

Time to think.

"Noah?" Dr. Odor's voice boomed. "You okay?"

"Be right out," Noah shouted.

"Take your time. We'll just set up the equipment."

Noah could hear voices coming through the bathroom door. He couldn't understand the words, but the pitch was different. Someone else was in on this crazy thing they put in his head.

Clenching the sides of the sink, he struggled to slow the pounding in his chest.

Should've kept quiet.

Should've asked Mom and Dad to stay.

But Dr. Odor said not to tell anyone.

He wondered what would happen if he did tell. Probably make his parents pay for the tests.

"Finished, Noah? We need to get the brain scan started."

Noah raised his head and stared into the mirror. "I'm just going to tell him, no. They can do their tests and then I'm done."

He flushed the stool, washed his hands, and opened the door. Three people were in the room waiting. Dr. Odor sat in the metal chair, tapping commands into his computer. A technician stood by the bed with an odd headset cradled in her hands. Noah grabbed the back of his gown when she smiled at him.

He glanced toward the third person and his muscles began to relax.

"Hey, Noah! You didn't lose that cheeseburger in there did you?" Lieutenant Green walked toward him with a can of soda in his hand. "Thought you might need a cold drink."

"Thanks," Noah said. He reached for the drink and wondered how much his new friend knew about the *experiments*. He opened the can and began chugging.

Dr. Odor glanced up from his screen. "I would suggest you not drink all of that. You won't be alert enough to get up in the night."

The thought of wetting the bed made heat crawl across his face. Noah stopped mid-swallow and set the partly filled can on the bedside table.

"Dr. Odor, I need to talk to you about what you said earlier," Noah said.

Dr. Odor's eyebrows arched. He shook his head. "We'll have to talk later. This test will take all night to complete and we need to get started." He turned to Lieutenant Green. "IV ready?"

"Right here." The lieutenant held up a clear bag with tubes and a needle.

Noah's body tensed.

"Good," said Dr. Odor. "Now, Noah, I want to explain as much as I can before you get sleepy." He motioned toward the bed.

Noah jumped onto the side of the bed while trying to hold the back of his gown. He pulled the sheet up to hide his skinny legs from three sets of eyes.

Dr. Odor smiled, then cleared his throat. "I'm going to simplify as much as I can. Stop me if you have questions." He pushed his glasses against his face. "The brain has billions and billions of active neurons. When they interact, there is a chemical reaction which emits electrical impulses. Following so far?"

Noah nodded and said, "I think so. When the brain works, there's a kind of electric snap you can see."

"Close enough." Dr. Odor nodded and continued. "The brain has folds in it that are different for each person."

"Like fingerprints?" Noah asked.

"Exactly!" The doctor looked pleased. "We want to see how the uniqueness of your brain affects the…uh…how your cochlear works."

That hesitation said the technician and Lieutenant Green might not know about the mind reading thing. Dr. Odor clicked his ink pen.

"Let's get the halo in position, then you can administer the sedative. Alright, Noah, I'll just take your processor," said Dr. Odor. "You won't need it during the test."

The silence was overwhelming. It made Noah feel out of control even more than before.

Lieutenant Green moved closer to the bed and gave a thumbs up, like he sensed Noah's uneasiness. A wide band was tied around his upper arm. Lieutenant Green showed Noah the needle and said, "Just a pinch."

Just a pinch? Right. Noah winced when the *pinch* burned like a bee sting on steroids.

Arm-like pads touched Noah's head in different places. It took several minutes for the tech to make sure the headset was in the correct position.

He thought it would make a great Halloween costume, like Frankenstein. He was about to ask for a mirror when the technician leaned in so Noah could read her lips.

"Try not to move around while you're going to sleep."

Noah breathed in her scent. It reminded him of his mom's perfume. Her kiss on his head before she left. Loneliness for his family overwhelmed him. He closed his eyes and tried to relax. Tried to think of how to tell the doctor he wasn't going to work for the government.

A plan was beginning to form when a fuzziness blurred his thoughts and sent him sliding, into nothing.

Chapter 9

Noah stretched and struggled to force his eyes open. The smell of bacon made his nose twitch.

A click on the side of Noah's head and hospital sounds blared like a squealing microphone. Lieutenant Green's smile filled his vision. "Hey, bud! Thought you were gonna sleep all day?"

The lieutenant stepped into the hall and brought back a food tray.

"Gotta go. Need the bathroom!" Noah said. His throat felt dry and sticky.

"Sure, kid." Lieutenant Green took his arm and helped him to stand. "Just take it easy. You might be a little dizzy."

Noah shuffle scooted to the bathroom. When he came out, Lieutenant Green was helping himself to something from Noah's tray.

"Oops! Caught me." He set the cover back on the plate. "Better eat. Doc wants to talk to you before your parents get here."

Noah felt a tingle in his head and then the lieutenant's thoughts. *Sure could use a cup of coffee.*

"You can go get coffee." Noah chugged the orange juice on the tray. "All I'm doing is eating."

Lieutenant Green smiled. "You read my thoughts, Noah. Be back in a few."

"Hmm," Noah mumbled. He didn't think the lieutenant knew about the mind reading thing but now he wasn't so sure. He wolfed down the bacon and half the eggs.

The overpowering smell of Dr. Odor's cologne reached him before he heard the tap, tap of the doctor's shoes in the hall. This might be the last chance he could say he wasn't going to work for the government. He rubbed his sweaty palms on the bed sheets and blew out a deep breath.

"Good morning, Noah!" The doctor shut the door and sat in the chair. "I trust you slept well."

"I guess," said Noah. "I don't remember anything, so I guess I did."

Dr. Odor's laugh boomed through Noah's cochlear.

"I need to talk to you," Noah said. "You know what you said about the tests and," Noah lowered his voice to a whisper, "about working for the government?" He pushed the rolling table away and hung his legs over the edge of the bed. "You can do the tests, but I don't want to work for the government. I'm only in the seventh grade!" He bit at a hang nail on the edge of his thumb. "I have to go to school, don't I?" For a minute he wondered if the government could change that.

"Ha, ha!" Dr. Odor laughed, his mouth so wide, Noah could see the fillings in his teeth. "Yes, we are aware you are still in school. No one wants to interfere with your education. Billings will explain everything in due time."

He stood and clicked his pen several times.

Ignored Noah's refusal.

"I need to remind you of the importance of not sharing any of this with your parents or friends."

"No problem with friends. Don't have any." Noah pretended it didn't matter, but it hurt when he heard himself say it in his robotic words.

"That's good." The doctor's forehead wrinkled. "I'm sorry. I didn't mean that the way it sounded. It just simplifies things."

Poor kid. We're going to make his life even more complicated.

"Ha! Complicated? Sounds crazy to me." Noah jumped from the bed. "Why am I supposed to trust you?"

"Hmm…" The doctor rubbed his mouth and chin. He moved toward Noah and again ignored the question. "I meant to switch the NT switch off on your processor." He reached behind Noah's ear and tapped the button. "No need to hear more than is necessary."

Noah was uncomfortable with how the doctor kept avoiding his questions. He touched the processor. "How did you do that so fast?"

"We made some modifications while we were doing your brain scan. We'll discuss that later." He picked up the phone, punched some numbers, and mumbled something into the mouthpiece. He set the phone onto the base and leaned close enough to make Noah wince from his coffee breath.

"I need to make sure you understand completely," he said softly. "I strongly encourage you to spend some time thinking about the opportunity this is for you and your family."

Noah squirmed in his seat.

Dr. Odor smiled and seemed happy about Noah's uneasiness. "Like I said earlier, it is imperative that you don't say anything to your parents about our plans. You don't want them harmed by things they don't need to know." The door opened, and Lieutenant Green popped his head around the corner.

"Ah, Lieutenant. We're going to let Noah get dressed. You can wait with him here, then bring him to my office." He clicked his pen three or four times. "I'll intercept his parents in the lobby and meet you there."

46

Two more clicks of his pen and he left.

"Well, Noah, my man. Looks like you finally get your pants back." He reached inside the closet and tossed Noah's jeans and shirt on the bed. "I'll take this tray and give you some privacy."

Noah stared at the closed door. Grabbed his clothes and ran to the bathroom. He dressed quickly, then slid down the wall and sat on the floor. It was too much. He wrapped his arms around his knees and rocked back and forth.

The doctor's words looped in his head as he tried to ignore knocks on the door.

Can't tell.

Harmed.

Don't want your parents harmed.

HARMED.

Chapter 10

"**S**o, Mr. and Mrs. Baker, I assure you we found no issues with Noah's implant. We have determined he was experiencing a sinus headache. Nothing more," said Dr. Odor.

A sinus headache? Sounded lame to Noah. He sat in a chair between his parents and did his sweaty palm thing.

Noah's dad scooted to the edge of his chair. "So, you're telling us it took an overnight hospital visit and who knows how many tests to decide he had a sinus headache? I hope our insurance will cover all this." He leaned onto his knees and rested his head in his hands.

"Remember? I told you in the clinic. There won't be a charge," Dr. Odor said. "The company was glad for the opportunity to do some tests involving the implant." He gave Noah a slight wink.

"So, I can go home. Right?" Noah asked.

He stood, hoping the meeting was over.

Could have bet it wasn't.

"Not yet, Noah." Dr. Odor opened a side drawer and pulled out a file folder. "I have a proposition to discuss with you and your parents."

Noah noticed his parents' quick glances toward each other as he sat back in his chair. He felt so disloyal to them. Didn't they have a right to know the rest of the story before they agreed to Dr. Odor's deal?

Dr. Odor pushed the folder toward them. "The company that manufactured your son's implant and the government are developing a community service program in conjunction with several disabled children's organizations. We would like to offer Noah the opportunity to work with us." The doctor looked to Noah's mom, his dad, then zeroed in on him. "Noah, we want you to be an ambassador representing the cochlear manufacturer."

Noah looked over his dad's shoulder at a kind of contract. His stomach went cold when he realized what was happening.

Work for the government.

Don't want them harmed by things they don't need to know.

"Why?" Noah's mom asked. "Why Noah?"

Mom seemed surprised that someone would want him to do an important job. Heat traveled up Noah's neck to his face. He realized she was right. If he hadn't been given the wrong cochlear, there was no way he would have been asked.

"Good question, Mrs. Baker." Dr. Odor cleared his throat and sat on the edge of the desk. "We've been looking for someone to do this job for some time. Your son is clever, he thinks on his feet, and..."

"I'm the only one who..."

Everyone jumped when a container of pencils and pens fell from the desk and crashed to the floor. Noah was positive the doctor pushed it on purpose. While the adults cleaned up the mess, Noah reached for the NT button on his cochlear. He found a small raised spot just under the surface. He pressed it and immediately heard Dr. Odor's thoughts.

Can't tell them. Not safe.

The doctor moved the container to a different spot on the desk. "As I was saying, we think Noah is the perfect age to serve at some public events we're planning."

"Events. What kind of events?" Mom asked. "It's difficult for me to get away from work and Noah and his dad will be back in school in less than a month."

"Don't remind me," Noah muttered.

Mom patted his knee.

"Aren't we jumping ahead of an obvious question?" Dad turned in his chair to face Noah. "Son, does this seem like something you would want to do?"

Dr. Odor stood. "Noah, before you answer that, let me give you additional information." He walked toward Noah. "It looks like your processor has come loose. Let me fix that for you."

Noah felt a click and knew the NT had been shut off.

Again—convenient.

The doctor returned to his chair. "There would be financial compensation for Noah's time. We're thinking expenses, plus a college scholarship fund. Of course, the company will cover all medical costs associated with your cochlear now and in the future." He hesitated and stared at Noah. "That is, if you serve as our ambassador and follow our requirements."

Noah caught the doctor's hidden meaning. No more worry about medical bills and college if he kept his mouth shut and did what they said.

"It's all included in the contract."

"Ya, right," Noah mumbled.

Mom reached over and squeezed Dad's hand. His parents had never said anything to him about money being tight, but he'd seen the stack of bills on Mom's desk.

Dr. Odor handed Mom another sheet of paper. "This is a preliminary schedule. As you see, the first event is this weekend here at the hospital. That's where we would introduce Noah to the board of directors and several other dignitaries. If that works well, the next event will be New York City in September."

Noah scooted to the front of his chair. "Excuse me. Could you repeat that? I thought you said New York."

"That's right, Noah. Some very important people are interested in our new cochlear Ambassador program."

"Wow!" Noah said. He pictured himself spitting off the top of the Empire State Building.

Dad leaned forward to the edge of his chair. "Sounds like an awesome opportunity. I think my principal might give me some time off to take you."

Noah could feel his dad's excitement. But dad didn't know the rest of the deal. Like, whose mind would he be asked to read? Some foreign leader? Someone in our own government? Noah bit his lip.

Dr. Odor clicked the pen in his hand. "I'm sorry I didn't explain further. There won't be time to receive clearance for either you or your wife to attend the function. Just Noah. Of course, we would provide him with a trusted chaperone." He pressed a button on the desk phone. "Lieutenant Green, we're ready for you." He leaned back in his chair and raised his eyebrows at Noah.

The door opened. "Mr. and Mrs. Baker, this is Lieutenant Nathan Green. He has been Noah's escort and nurse while he's been in the hospital."

The lieutenant shook Noah's parents' hands. "It's a pleasure to meet both of you." He sat in a chair facing them and gave Noah a quick salute.

"Lieutenant Green and Noah have become fast friends. He'll be with your son at all events to make sure he is safe and healthy."

The doctor's pen clicks echoed under his desk.

Noah liked the idea of spending more time with the lieutenant. But it kind of felt like having a babysitter.

"This is a lot for us to digest, Doctor." Dad flipped through the pages in his hand.

Noah was frustrated when Mom mumbled something Noah couldn't understand. She reached across him to touch Dad's arm. Then she said, "Could we take this home to discuss? We can let you know our decision tomorrow."

Dr. Odor stood and walked around the desk. "Of course. Here's my card if you have questions." He opened the office door. "I'll need a call from you within the next twenty-four hours."

Noah's mind screamed inside his head. Going to New York sounded cool but things were happening way too fast. His heart throbbed in his throat.

Dr. Odor's heels clicked on the tile floor as he led them down the hall. "Oh, one more thing. I hate to keep you longer, but I want to check Noah's processor to see why it came loose earlier. Lieutenant Green will take you to the lobby and Noah and I will meet you there."

Noah's mind was racing. How could he keep the truth from his mom and dad? If they knew the whole story about the implant goof, they would have said no immediately. Even if the money was tempting.

"Noah, let's just step into this exam room where we can talk." The doctor gestured for Noah to go first into the room then shut the door behind them. He set his clipboard on the counter. "Have a seat. We have a little bit of time. I instructed Lieutenant Green to take the long way to the lobby."

Noah didn't sit but let the questions fly. "Why aren't you telling my parents the truth? Do you really want me to go to New York or is that a lie too?"

Dr. Odor raised his palms like a crossing guard. "We don't have time to go into all that right now. Have a seat. I need to give you some instructions before we meet your parents."

"I'll sit, but I want to know why my parents and I have to do what you say."

"Ha, ha!" The doctor's laughter boomed. "It's that kind of spirit that helps me know you will be perfect for the job we need you to do."

"You didn't answer my question."

"Okay." The doctor rubbed the back of his neck. "I was hoping to wait for you to talk to Captain Billings, but I can see it won't wait."

Noah's stomach twisted. He fought the urge to move toward the door when the doctor moved his chair close.

"Noah, your ability with this special implant is remarkable. You can do something very special to help your country." Dr. Odor leaned in close and spoke in a whisper like he was afraid someone was eavesdropping. "But there are other people who would be interested in using your abilities as well. Bad people. Do you understand?"

Noah stared at his feet. Counted the lace holes in his shoes. Ten on each foot.

Dr. Odor cleared his throat and said again, "Noah? Do you understand?"

Noah looked up and took a deep breath. "So, you're saying bad people would want to hurt my family?" He felt bile burn in his throat.

"Yes," said Dr. Odor. "Your life and the lives of your family depend on your cooperation."

Noah bolted for the nearest trashcan.

Chapter 11

T he hum of the elevator almost hypnotized Noah as he watched
the digital display tick off the floor numbers. An electrical
smell mixed with the doctor's cologne made the rest of his
breakfast close to reappearing.

"I trust you're feeling better now." Dr. Odor didn't wait for him
to respond. "When you get home, we want you to practice with the
NT," the doctor said, "but only for short periods of time. We're not
completely sure what the effects of long-term usage will be."

Long-term effects?

And who is WE?

Dr. Odor cleared his throat and said, "When you come back to
the hospital on Saturday, we'll give you more instructions." He pulled
his phone from his pocket when it dinged. "Oh, and make sure you
convince your parents you want this."

"What if I don't want it?" Noah whispered to himself.

BAD people.

Can't tell anyone.

The elevator doors opened. Noah saw his parents waiting beside
Lieutenant Green. He fought the urge to run straight into his mom's
arms.

Dr. Odor straightened his tie and gestured for Noah to go first. The robotic sound of the doctor's clicking steps echoed behind him.

"Mr. & Mrs. Baker," The doctor moved ahead of Noah and extended his right hand. "I'm sorry for keeping you."

Dad grabbed the doctor's hand. "No problem, Doctor. We appreciate this opportunity for Noah. Oh, and thank you for giving us time to make the decision."

Noah glanced at the faces of the three adults.

Opportunity?

If Dad only knew.

The doctor focused on Noah while he looked over the top of his glasses. He cleared his throat again and said, "We'll be waiting for a call with your decision."

* * * * * *

Once they were in the car, Noah removed his cochlear, wanting quiet to think through the conversation with Dr. Odor. It was so crazy! How could he go from being a frustrated deaf kid to a character in a spy novel in just a few days?

He thought about the bills on mom's desk. About the scholarship Dr. Odor said they would give him for college.

Bad people.

Dangerous.

What would happen if the bad people found out about his cochlear?

Would he live long enough to go to college?

And most of all…who was in the black SUV that had been on their bumper since they left the hospital?

Noah covered his face with his hands. He needed to tell someone.

He looked up when he felt the car slow and pull into their driveway.

Mom turned in her seat. She exaggerated her words, so he could read her lips. "Let's go inside and talk."

Noah nodded and replaced the processor. He stepped from the car and followed his parents into the house.

Tod was waiting in the front hall. "Where have you been? I'm starved!"

Maybe he could talk to Tod. Then his brother rammed him with his shoulder and Noah knew Tod would never believe him. Probably make a big joke of it with his jerk friends.

"We need a family meeting." Dad headed to the kitchen. The rest of the family followed. Even Tod.

Noah clicked the NT button. Everyone's thought words rushed at him so fast it took his breath. He reached to shut it off but stopped himself. Didn't want to guess what his parents were thinking.

He needed to know.

Chapter 12

D ad turned his chair backwards and straddled the seat. Noah sat across from his mom and watched her rearrange the salt and pepper in the middle of the table. Tod leaned against the doorframe. Arms crossed, staring out the window with a scowl.

No one said a word, but their thoughts were running over one another in Noah's head.

You're going to ruin that chair.

How do we decide this?

Get this over so we can eat.

Should I fix lunch?

I hate family meetings.

Noah covered his ears with his hands. "EVERYONE STOP TALKING!" He didn't think he'd said it out loud, but they all stared at him. "Sorry," he said. "I meant, everyone start talking."

Mom leaned across the table and touched Noah's hand. "Okay. What do you want to do?"

Dad walked to the fridge. "Yes, we need to know your honest opinion about doing this ambassador thing." He grabbed bottles of water and brought them to the table. "Where's that contract Dr. Odor gave us?"

Mom rummaged through her purse. "Here." She smoothed the papers with fingers Noah knew were icy.

"What's all this about? What contract?" Tod asked.

"I'm glad you're finally interested, Tod," Dad said. "Sit down and we'll explain."

Dad repeated all the things that had happened since Noah's trip to the hospital.

Everything except the parts Dad didn't know. Like spy stuff and danger to their family.

"So!" Tod blurted out. "Little brother's going to be a big shot. What's that got to do with me?" He tipped back in his chair.

Mom left the kitchen and brought back a stack of papers. "This is how it affects you, Tod Baker." She slammed the stack on the table. "Insurance paid for most of Noah's surgery, but we've met our maximum benefit. We never intended on moving but we didn't have a choice. The house payment is higher, utilities, property taxes, car payments. Everything costs more here. We're having to dip into our savings. Savings intended for college for you boys."

Dad reached for Mom's arm. She jerked away.

"I'm sorry, Mom," Noah said. "I didn't know."

She stood and put her arms around Noah's shoulders. "It's not your fault, son."

Tod's thoughts shouted in Noah's head. *Why don't you just say it! It's my fault! I was a jerk to make you get my phone. It should have been me who hit the windshield.*

Noah snapped his head toward Tod and their eyes met.

"Why are you looking at me, freak?"

Tod's words didn't match the hurt in his thoughts.

Dad flicked through the papers, ignoring Tod's insult. "If I understand this contract correctly," he said, "all Noah's medical expenses could be paid."

"And college?" Mom stood and looked over Dad's shoulder. "That amount can't be right." She pointed at the page.

Dad whistled. "With just a couple events, your first year of college would be covered."

Noah squirmed in his seat. "That's if I do what they want me to do."

"That's right, Noah. These events will keep you from other activities," said Dad.

Noah snorted and said, "What activities?"

Dad's face flushed. "I know you haven't been able to do things like you used to, but that doesn't mean you can't in the future."

Noah hadn't let himself think about the future since the accident. Maybe he could do something besides go to doctor's appointments and school.

Like work for the government?

Noah touched Mom's hand and sensed her thoughts coming to him.

Wonderful opportunity for my baby.

Noah rolled his eyes and pulled his hand away. He glanced at Tod, then Dad. Tod looked bored. Dad, hopeful.

"We'd better read the rest of the contract before we decide for sure," Mom said.

Dad nodded and popped his knuckles.

Tod slammed his chair to all four legs. "Seriously? Can't we eat first?"

Dad reached for the contract and said, "You're almost seventeen years old! Make your own sandwich."

Not what I had in mind.

Noah smirked at his brother's secret thoughts, then stopped. As much as he celebrated when his brother got yelled at, deep down he wouldn't want him hurt. Put in danger because his little brother was a chicken. His parents either.

Dr. Odor's warnings hammered at him.
Your family's safety. Your safety. Convince them.
CONVINCE THEM.

Chapter 13

Noah had told his parents he needed time to think. He stayed in his room longer than he probably should have but finally came back to the kitchen. Mom's eyes were red like she'd been crying. The guilt of knowing he again caused her pain tore at him. He closed his eyes and searched for his parents' thoughts. A battle of whispers tumbled in his brain so fast none of it made sense. He took a deep breath and concentrated on the bits and pieces of his mom's voice first. Slowly it was like one thread floated to the top.

You're not strong enough. Too much responsibility. Need to take care of you.

Noah's eyes flew open and landed on Mom's face.

"This could be that new beginning we talked about," she said. She was smiling but her true thoughts made him question every good thing she'd ever said about him.

"This is your choice, Noah," Dad said. "Your mom and I discussed it when you took a break earlier and whatever you decide we'll support." He held his open palms in front of him like he was resigning from the decision.

"Noah," Dad said a little stronger.

"Give me a minute," Noah said.

He walked to the cabinet and grabbed a glass even though his bottle was half full on the table. He stared out the window at the neighbor's cat stalking a bird. Pictured the cat as Dr. Odor and him as the bird. He closed his eyes. Searched for Dad's mind words.

Come on. Be a man.

Bankruptcy would destroy us.

Noah cringed at the truth he heard. Dad's "be a man" speech was usually aimed at Tod. Bankruptcy wasn't a word he understood but he knew it had to do with money and that it was bad.

CONVINCE THEM.

Glad Tod was dismissed earlier to go lift weights with his friends, Noah prepared himself to tell one of the biggest lies he had ever told his parents. Knew Tod would see right through it. Prayed his parents couldn't.

"I'll do it," Noah said, then forced a smile. He turned to his mom. "I can do this."

Mom's cheeks glowed red as her eyes darted from Dad back to Noah. "Of course, you can. We're sure of that," she said.

Yeah right, Noah thought. He regretted hearing their true feelings. Scratched his head and pressed the NT button off. With the barrage of real sounding brain words silenced, he could concentrate on the robot talk coming through his cochlear.

Dad stood. "If you're sure, son." He turned his chair the right way and pushed it under the table edge. Didn't wait for Noah's agreement. "We better call the doctor."

* * * * * *

An hour after the contract was signed and the call was made to the doctor, a military vehicle pulled to the curb in front of the Baker house. A driver in uniform saluted when Dad opened the door.

"Good afternoon, sir." The soldier stood in the doorway at full attention. "Dr. Odor sent me to collect the paperwork you have for him."

"Of course." Dad cleared his throat and looked at Mom. "Come in."

"Sorry they're so wrinkled," Dad said as he handed the papers to the soldier. "We read them several times."

"No problem, sir." The soldier transferred the contract to an official looking briefcase. "Noah, to protect your private information, please press your thumb print on this spot."

Noah hesitated but pressed the spot and heard the case lock.

It locked—with his thumb print! His stomach took a dive. What was the government's plan for him that needed a locked briefcase? And how the heck did they get his thumb print?

Mom and Dad exchanged questioning looks. Dad stepped forward. Noah was sure he was about to question the soldier further.

CONVINCE THEM.

Noah needed a distraction.

"Hey," he said to the soldier, "what does that patch stand for?" he pointed to the man's arm.

"That's a combat patch for my deployments overseas."

Noah could tell the man was pleased he asked but instead of giving details, he slipped a manila envelope from under his arm and handed it to him.

"Everything needed for the…uh… next step is included in this envelope."

Noah was sure the soldier was going to say MISSION. Glad he didn't.

"If you have questions, call the number provided. Have a good day."

Before his parents could say anymore, the soldier jogged toward the waiting car.

Mom blew out her breath like she'd been holding it. "Why is the military so involved?" She put her arm around Noah's shoulders. The coldness of her hands soaked through his shirt. "And why is it addressed to you, Noah?" She sounded surprised.

Noah remembered her thoughts…*not strong enough.* He pulled away from her arm and headed for the stairs.

"You better open it, don't you think?" Dad said.

Noah wanted to go to his room to read it but didn't want to make his parents any more suspicious. He sat on the bottom step and opened the fastener. A typed note on cream colored paper fell to the floor.

The front door flew open and Tod was home from weightlifting.

Noah turned the paper over and over in his hands, hoping Tod would keep walking out of the room. Instead, his brother plopped onto the couch across the room but near enough to hear everything.

"Would you like me to read it for you?" Mom asked.

"No!" he said way too strong. "I'm not a baby." He wished he hadn't pressed the NT button to hear his parents' thoughts after all. This mind reading stuff wasn't nearly as cool as he thought it would be.

Mouth dry, Noah read the note out loud.

MEMORANDUM FOR: NOAH HENRY BAKER
SUBJECT: NOTICE OF EVENT PARTICIPATION &
TRAINING

1. THIS DOCUMENT IS TO CONFIRM CLEARANCE TO PARTICIPATE IN PROJECT *DO YOU HEAR WHAT I HEAR* (DYH). TRAINING WITH DR. IVAN ODOR AND PERSONEL.
2. NOAH HENRY BAKER ID # 9988123 STATUS: COCHLEAR AMBASSADOR

3. THIS EVENT REQUIRES THE FOLLOWING:
   - BUSINESS CASUAL WITH LEATHER SHOES (Company shirt will be provided)
   - ACCOMPANIMENT WITH APPROVED CHAPERONE: Lieutenant Nathan Green
   - PARTICIPATION IN ALL MEETINGS AND TRAINING
4. APPROVED CHAPERONE AND DRIVER WILL TRANSPORT PARTICIPANT FROM PARTICIPANT'S RESIDENCE TO WALTER REED NATIONAL MILITARY MEDICAL CENTER AT 0800 HOURS ON SATURDAY, 28 July.
5. FURTHER INQUIRIES: CONTACT DR. IVAN ODOR AT WALTER REED, Extension #8123.

CAPTAIN, JAMES H. BILLINGS, MILITARY INTELLIGENCE OFFICER (MIO)

The name BILLINGS jumped out at Noah…Billings will explain…

"How did they know my middle name and when is 0800 hours?" Noah asked. He peeked in the big envelope and pulled out a yellow gold shirt with the cochlear logo on the front.

"I have a feeling they know lots of things," Mom said as she took the shirt and held it up. "This looks a little big." She held it against Noah's chest before continuing, "I still don't understand why the military is involved with the cochlear people."

CONVINCE THEM.

"All the tests were at the military hospital," said Noah. "Maybe that's where they have their board meetings." He literally bit down on his tongue to keep from saying more. Couldn't say they had signed his life away to the government.

"It's 8 a.m.," Tod said from the couch. "0800 hours, is eight in the morning. Military time."

"How did you know that?" Noah asked.

Tod shrugged. "Dorky shirt," he said, and headed to the kitchen.

"Does Noah even own leather shoes that fit?" Dad asked.

"No," Mom said. She grabbed her purse from the chair. "Probably needs a new pair of khakis too."

Noah turned the envelope and dumped out a plastic card. "Here's a pre-paid cash card." He noticed the silent communication between his parents.

"Let's go before the mall closes," Mom said. She pulled her keys from her purse and checked her hair in the mirror by the door.

Noah rolled his eyes. He hated shopping with his mom. She always told him to choose what he wanted then bought what she wanted him to have. He scrubbed his sweaty palms on his shorts and opened the front door.

The sun was sinking lower in the sky as Noah walked toward the passenger side of Mom's car. The scent of grilled meat hovered in the air from the neighbor's backyard. It reminded him of the cookout his ball team gave him to say goodbye. The one where most of the guys ignored him, not knowing what to say to a deaf kid. What would they say if they knew he was going to work for the government? He'd turn on the NT and hear their real thoughts—or maybe not.

Noah turned toward the car and almost swallowed his gum when he noticed a black SUV parked down the street.

The same one that followed them from the hospital.

Chapter 14

Noah startled when Mom honked her car horn. She rolled down the passenger window beside where he stood. "What are you waiting for, Noah. We need to go!"

"Sorry. Just thinking."

Before he crawled into the passenger seat, Noah glanced at the black car still parked in front of the vacant house two doors down. Mom backed onto the street. He kept his eyes on the vehicle behind them through the side mirror. Shiny black finish, dark windows, no license plate on the front bumper. He was kind of proud of himself for starting to act like a real spy who notices everything.

Noah released his breath when the vehicle stayed planted at the curb. Must have been his imagination. Wouldn't Dr. Odor have said something if someone was going to follow them?

"What's the matter?" Mom asked. She swiveled her head back and forth from watching the road.

Noah cleared his throat. Wished he could tell her like he would have when he was little.

"Nothing. Just kind of nervous about this Ambassador thing, I guess."

"Well, that's to be expected," she said. "You'll be great!"

Even without the NT active, he knew that wasn't what she really thought.

"Just remember to be polite," she said, "shake hands like we've taught you, and don't talk with your mouth full."

Noah huffed out his breath. Typical mom advice. The only thing she left out was to wear clean underwear. He relaxed into the seat and watched the houses of their neighborhood slide by. A flicker caught his attention in the side mirror. The SUV had moved into the street behind them. His heart pulsed in his throat.

Mom turned right at the stop light.

The SUV turned right at the stop light.

Mom moved to the center lane.

The SUV moved to the center lane.

"Mom, can you pull into the Mini-Mart? I want a Pepsi."

"Let's get something at the mall, sweetie," she said.

"Can't wait." He faked a cough. "My treat."

Mom smiled and flipped on the turn signal. "OK. Since you're buying, make mine a large." She steered into a parking space. Noah was out the door before she shut off the engine.

"You wait here. It'll be faster."

As much as Noah didn't want to hear his mom's thoughts, he pressed the NT button in case he needed it with the people in the black car. He trotted into the crowded store through the automatic doors. The aroma of fresh popcorn just barely covered the smell of floor cleaner. He slipped around the wet floor sign then pretended to study souvenir magnets on display near the front window. The SUV weaved through the busy parking lot. When the passenger door on the vehicle opened, Noah moved to the drink dispenser. He pretended calmness while he filled two large drinks. The automatic doors dinged and a guy in a *Men in Black* suit and sunglasses walked through the front door.

"Way to blend into the crowd," Noah mumbled. He ducked behind another display then moved to the checkout counter.

"That'll be $4.50," said the girl at the counter. Then she mumbled something.

"What did you say?" Noah asked. He was surprised he couldn't read her thoughts.

The girl's eyes went to Noah's cochlear and she raised her voice loud. All heads in the store swiveled in their direction. He ducked his head and slid a five onto the counter.

"Would you like to donate your change to St. Jude's Children's Hospital?"

"Yeah, sure," Noah said and bolted for the door.

He handed Mom her drink through the open car window and glanced back and forth from the store to the SUV. Sweat dripped and stung his eyes.

"We'd better get going," Noah said.

He wanted to tell her to floor it.

Kept his voice calm instead.

"Just need a quick drink first," Mom said and took a long pull on the straw. "Oh, that's good." She sat the cup in the holder and turned the key.

Noah caught a glimpse of the sunglasses guy running to the SUV. "Can you drive faster, Mom? You said the mall closes in a couple hours."

"Now you're in a hurry?" She put the car in reverse and kept talking. He looked in the side mirror and smiled. Suit guy's vehicle was blocked by other cars waiting for the gas pumps.

"Did you hear me, Noah?" Mom asked.

He struggled to understand her robotic words.

"I'm so proud of you, Noah."

"Such an honor."

Been a horrible year...Hope we aren't pressing you too hard.

"I need to call your grandparents and tell them all about it."

Need to do laundry when I get home.

Noah covered his ears and shouted, "One thing at a time!"

Eyes wide, Mom stepped on the brake. "What's wrong? Are you in pain?"

Maybe I better take him back to Dr. Odor.

"Sorry, Mom. All the sound makes me crazy sometimes. You know. Because I don't get all the words." He switched off the NT.

"Of course."

He saw the hurt in her eyes. For the umpteeth time he wished he could explain.

She sniffed and said, "I'll just turn on some music and not talk for a while."

The hissing beats and unrecognizable lyrics were annoying but at least he couldn't hear the *mom think-talk*. He turned down the volume on his cochlear and gulped from his cup. The side mirror caught his attention. He searched for the black vehicle that still wasn't in view.

Mom turned into the mall entrance and parked outside *her* favorite store. She grabbed her purse and checked her hair in the mirror one more time. "Feeling better?" she asked.

Noah nodded and unbuckled his seat belt. The black SUV drove by them and parked. Something clicked in him. How did they know where he and his mom had driven when they were so far behind? Noah's fist came down hard on the arm rest and he shot out the door.

He ignored Mom's robotic shouts behind him.

Noah sprinted across the parking lot and hid behind cars until he was behind the idling black vehicle. He wasn't sure what his plan was, but he had to know who these guys were. The car's exhaust fumes choked him as he turned up the volume on his cochlear microphone. On the passenger's side, a red-shirted arm flicked a brown cigarette.

Were government guys supposed to smoke on duty?

Noah's fingers slid across the sun heated surface of the dark paint. One step at a time, he pretended he was on a mission as he made his way to the front.

"Hey!" he hollered when he was beside the door. "Why are you following us?"

The guy in the passenger's seat dropped his cigarette then shouted something Noah couldn't understand. The car roared away so fast Noah jumped back to avoid having his foot crushed.

He didn't find out who they were, but he got a good look at the man. The brown cigarette still lay smoldering at his feet.

"Noah, Noah!" Mom hollered and grabbed his arm.

The SUV's tires squealed as the vehicle raced through the exit and onto the street.

Mom's scratchy words pulled at him and he lost sight of the car. "Noah, what are you doing?!"

"Oh, sorry, Mom," he said. "I thought that was someone I knew, but I guess not."

"You can't just walk up to any strange car you see. It's not safe."

Not safe. Noah wanted to laugh.

"I know. I'm sorry. I'll be more careful."

Ha! Careful while I do some kind of spy stuff.

Noah couldn't wait to ask Dr. Odor about the black car and the government guy with the red shirt.

Chapter 15

…0800 hours…

No visible SUV lurked in the neighborhood.

Noah watched from the window for the government car the instructions said would transport him back to Walter Reed. His mom fussing with his hair made him even more nervous than he already was. He wanted to shove her hand from his head, but he didn't. Instead, he kneeled to check his shoelaces. Turned to the nearby chair to unzip his backpack.

"I still don't feel good about you going without us," Mom said. She followed him and picked non-existent lint from the sleeve of the cochlear-logoed shirt Noah was required to wear.

"He's going to be fine," Dad said. "Let him enjoy this."

Back to the window, Noah watched a car with military tags stop in front of their house. Lieutenant Green exited the passenger side of the vehicle and jogged up the sidewalk.

Noah grabbed his backpack and opened the door before the lieutenant could ring the bell.

"Morning, Noah. Ready to go?"

"You bet." Noah looped one strap of his backpack across his shoulder and hollered to his parents, "Bye, Mom. Bye, Dad." He slammed the door behind him before his mom could do the teary thing that had been building all morning.

"Let's go," he said.

The neighbor's Pomeranian yipped at them in a machine-like pitch. The scent of mowed grass was strong. The sky, blue and cloudless. Would've been a perfect day for baseball practice. Before the accident. Always before and after.

"I've got a little surprise for you in the car." Lieutenant Green pulled open the back door and made an "after you" motion with his hand.

Noah imagined it was some kind of spy equipment. Maybe x-ray glasses or a cool new phone with top secret features.

The sun's glare made him squint and his eyes watered. The dark shape of someone on the far side of the seat told him he probably wasn't getting a new phone. He couldn't tell who it was but was sure it wasn't Dr. Odor because of the small size. Didn't know—until his head dipped low to slide onto the seat and he heard the robotic pop.

Smelled grape gum.

"Why are we picking up him?" the mysterious girl from the hospital said. "I thought I was the only freak you guys wanted to use."

Noah blinked repeatedly. Hoped the girl didn't think he was crying.

Lieutenant Green poked his head inside the car. "You kids get acquainted. Doc will explain the rest."

Noah felt the brain tingle.

That's what you always say.

"That's exactly what I was thinking." Noah smiled and leaned back into the seat. Glad he'd thought to turn on the NT.

The girl's eyes looked surprised. "What are you talking about, weirdo? I didn't say anything."

Noah cleared his throat. "Just thinking out loud, I guess. Sorry."

She blew a bubble and it popped onto her face.

Noah smiled and smothered the laugh that was building inside him. The girl's thought words hollered in his head.

Don't even think about laughing.

He watched the girl peel bits of purple from her lips and cheek. She turned with an exaggerated huff and faced the window.

Noah reached for his cochlear and shut off the NT button. Decided it might be better not to hear the thoughts of this interesting but scary girl.

"Buckle up, Noah, and I'll make introductions." Lieutenant Green pulled down the visor mirror from the passenger side and talked to them through the reflection. "This is MOS 88-M, Corporal Powell."

The driver did a quick two-finger salute and checked her mirrors before she turned the car onto the street.

"What's MOS-88-M stand for?" Noah asked.

Before either of the adults could answer, the girl beside him said, "Military Motor Transport Operator: Operate all wheel vehicles and equipment over varied terrain and roadways. Manage load, unload, and safety of personnel being transported. Employ convoy defense techniques."

No one spoke for a few seconds. Noah glanced from the girl to Lieutenant Green and Corporal Powell.

"How do you know all that?" Noah asked.

The girl held up her purple phone and waved it toward him. "I read. You ought to try it."

The lieutenant cleared his throat then said, "Noah Baker, meet Lena Robinson. She has a… great memory."

The girl rolled her eyes and turned to Noah. "Pu-lease! It's not just a great memory. I have an eidetic memory. Look it up." She faced the window and blew another bubble.

"What are you so mad about? It's not my fault you lost your leg." As soon as the words were out, Noah knew he'd stepped over some kind of line. Lena's eyes went from wounded Bambi to scary Cruella deVille in a split second.

"Okay, kids," said the lieutenant. "Let's just calm down. How about some tunes? You've got headphones back there to plug in your devices. Don't imagine you could agree on the same music."

Lena immediately jammed the earphones onto her head and popped three or four bubbles inside her mouth.

Since hissing pitches through the cochlear were just plain annoying, Noah opted to shut off all sound. The silence relaxed him, but he stewed about things the doctor had not bothered telling him—like the black SUV and how Lena fits into this spy thing. His brain wouldn't quit looping questions over and over. Questions he couldn't wait to ask Dr. Odor.

Chapter 16

*…0900 hours… **DO YOU HEAR WHAT I HEAR** (DYH).*

NOAH HENRY BAKER
ID # 9988123
STATUS: DYH in Training
(Alias: COCHLEAR AMBASSADOR)

Noah gripped the thick white notebook in sweaty fingers. Tried to ignore Lena beside him in Dr. Odor's office but was curious what her pages said.

"Lena, I'm sorry for what I said in the car. You know. About your leg."

She whipped her head toward him. Her eyes told him he was not forgiven.

Clicking steps sounded in the hall. Noah caught the abrasive scent of Dr. Odor's aftershave before he heard his words.

"Good morning, Noah, Lena." The doctor stood behind his desk then dropped into the chair. "I hope you've gotten to know one another. I'm sure you'll soon be great friends."

Noah could almost hear the eye roll from the girl beside him. As intimidating as Lena was, he was relieved to have another kid involved. Maybe they *could* be friends. He glanced at Lena and was rewarded with a Tod-like sneer.

Maybe not.

"I see you have your manuals. For now, you'll be training separately, but there are a few details that need explanation before we begin the process."

Noah squirmed in his seat. Wondered if Lena was being followed too.

"Dr. Odor," Noah said, "I need to ask you some questions about…"

The doctor interrupted, "We'll take care of questions later, Noah. For now, we have some details we need to cover before Captain Billings joins us."

Dr. Odor clicked his pen, Lena popped three bubbles in her mouth, and Noah rubbed his palms on his pant legs.

"Both of you have disabilities that have changed your lives. But those very disabilities fit perfectly into our plans. You will be posing as ambassadors for different organizations. Noah for the cochlear Association of America and Lena for the National Amputee Association."

Noah saw Lena's knuckles turn white as she squeezed the arms of her chair. He wondered what happened. Did she lose her leg in an accident or was it cut off in surgery? He shivered at either possibility. Forced himself not to look at her leg.

"Besides your disabilities, you both possess extraordinary talents that will help you fulfill the missions you will be assigned. This will take teamwork and a great deal of practice."

"What can he do that I can't do by myself?" Lena popped more bubbles until Dr. Odor held out a trashcan for the gum.

"That's what I'm about to explain." Dr. Odor set the trashcan on the floor and then picked up a paper from his desk. He read a list of numbers. "Noah, could you repeat those numbers back to me?"

Uh…uh…" Noah stuttered. "No, how could anyone remember that?" Heat traveled up his neck.

"Lena?"

"18964452784599123987564160."

"Correct!" Dr. Odor's laugh filled the room. Noah instinctively held his hand over his ears. Even the silent one.

"How did she do that?" He turned to Lena. "How did you do that?"

"I told you. Eidetic memory. I remember everything."

"Everything?"

"Everything. You walked twenty-six steps from your house to the car. The elevator ride took twenty-three point two seconds to arrive on this floor. We walked one hundred fifty-two steps to Dr. Odor's office. Antarctica is the only continent without reptiles or snakes. The color of the first bubble gum was pink because it was the only color the inventor had available."

"Okay, Lena. Enough for now." Dr. Odor walked around the desk and stood in front of Noah.

"Is the neurological transmissions processor active?"

"No." Noah said. "I shut it off in the car." He glanced at Lena and gave his own *you better not mess with me* stare.

"May I?" Dr. Odor reached behind Noah's ear. "Have you been practicing?"

"Some. Seems like it works better when the person I'm listening to is either happy or mad. You know, emotional." He glanced at Lena.

"Interesting," Dr. Odor said. "Now, Lena, I want you to think of what you ate for breakfast."

"Why? That's weird," she said.

"Just humor me, please. What did you have for breakfast?"

Noah felt a head tingle and the words came through.

Scrambled tofu and turkey bacon.

"Gross! Who eats scrambled tofu? Oh, and bacon...turkey bacon."

"How did you know that?" Lena turned to Dr. Odor. "Do you have cameras in my house?" She stood and wobbled a little.

The doctor frowned. "Of course we don't have cameras in your house. Just sit and I'll explain." Then he gave Lena all the information about Noah's implant and his brain.

"So, he can read my thoughts right now? That's creepy. Shut it off. Now!"

"Noah," Dr. Odor said.

Noah reached behind his ear and pressed the button. "It's off."

"As I've told both of you," the doctor clicked his pen, "all of this is top secret. You've agreed not to tell anyone. It is imperative that you follow through on your agreement." He stared intently at Lena then Noah. "Do you both understand?"

"Yes, sir," Noah said.

Lena nodded.

"Good!" Dr. Odor opened his own notebook and said, "Let's begin."

The next hour was an introduction to the two organizations they would be representing. Names, dates, history of the organizations. There were also lists of acronyms for various parts of the government that they were told to memorize.

"No problem," said Lena.

Noah groaned when he looked through the list. "Homework? We have homework?" He hated the whine in his voice. Knew he sounded like a little kid.

There were a couple things he remembered. MOS-88-M was the code for Corporal Powell's job. NT was the abbreviation for the special feature his cochlear had. But there were probably a hundred more.

"Don't worry," Lena said. "I'll help you."

"I don't need your help," he mumbled.

"Yes, you do," Dr. Odor said. "You are going to have to learn to help one another. To trust the skills you each possess."

Lena slumped in her seat and crossed her arms. "Why do we have to work together? I'm better as a solo."

"I was wondering the same thing," Noah said. "How can she help me read minds? And whose thoughts am I supposed to hear?"

Dr. Odor leaned forward in his chair. "Those are not details I've been told." He flipped a few pages. "Now, if you'll turn to page eighty-five, you'll find your speeches for this afternoon."

"Speeches?!" Noah tore through the pages, hoping he had misunderstood. "Oh, man," he said when he found it. He scrubbed his hands on his pants. All his past failures while standing in front of his class scrolled through his brain.

"I don't do speeches," he said.

"You'll be fine," Dr. Odor said.

Typical grown-up speak.

Dr. Odor stood and pressed a button on his desk. "We have speech coaches ready to help you individually prepare for this afternoon."

The door opened.

"Lieutenant Green, Lena and Noah are ready to begin their coaching sessions."

"Yes, sir," said the lieutenant. "Follow me and try to keep up."

Noah smelled grape gum and knew Lena had replaced the piece she'd been forced to drop in the trash. Three quick pops confirmed it.

"I don't do speeches," Noah said again.

"I guess you do now, soldier."

Chapter 17

…14:00… Introduction of Ambassadors

The sweet scent of flowers on the portable stage made it impossible for Noah to get a deep breath without a wave of *puke-itus*. A static hum of voices filled the meeting room and only added to terror building with each second. He folded and unfolded his speech until the sweat from his hands made it damp.

"Just relax, Noah," Lena whispered. "You want us to look like a couple of kids?"

"We are a couple of kids!" Noah hissed.

"True," she said through clenched teeth, "but didn't your speech coach tell you we had to convince these people that we are the best for the job?"

"What?" More panic. "No! We spent most of our time trying to figure out ways to ignore the audience and get the words out."

Noah opened his palm and showed Lena a paperclip that had left an impression in his hand. "This is supposed to distract me from the hundreds of eyes watching me fail."

"Does it work?" Lena asked.

"What do you think?" Noah said and moaned as he slumped in his chair.

"Just smile and pretend you want to be here," she said, then flipped her hair and did a little wave at the crowd.

"Ladies and gentlemen," Dr. Odor said in his booming voice, "thank you for gathering with us today. Without any further delay, I'd like to introduce you to the newest representatives of our organizations."

He turned and pointed to Lena with his extended arm. "Lena Robinson is the new Children's Ambassador of the National Amputee Association. Lena lost her leg in a boating accident when her body came in contact with the propeller."

Noah's head rotated to Lena before he could stop himself. He imagined the blood in the water—the terror she must have felt. The pain. His stomach lurched. He was tempted to put his arm around her shoulders. Knew her reaction wouldn't be a good thing. More like an injured cat exposing her claws.

"Lena has been fitted with the latest and best prosthesis science can offer. Before the accident, she was an award-winning runner and swimmer at her school. She'll work toward pursuing both sports again. Welcome, Lena Robinson."

Noah wondered if Dr. Odor had convinced her she would run again if she cooperated.

Lena stood and walked to the podium. If Noah hadn't known about her leg, he wouldn't have noticed the slight wobble in her steps. He watched her face on the large screen in the back of the room. She was good at this kind of thing, really good. The adults sitting at the cloth covered tables were captivated by her memorized speech.

It sure didn't help Noah feel secure in his speech-reading ability.

Lena turned away from the crowd and glared at Noah as she walked back to her seat.

It felt like the bones in Noah's legs had dissolved. He wondered if he could trust them to get him to the podium. Dr. Odor's words came in a roar through his cochlear.

"Noah Baker will be the Children's Ambassador of the cochlear Association of America. Noah lost hearing in both ears due to a head injury in a car accident. He is a fighter and has made tremendous progress adjusting to life with a cochlear implant. Welcome, Noah Baker."

Noah scrubbed his palms on his thighs and stood. His trembling legs did get him to the podium where he smoothed wrinkles from the speech he'd been practicing. He began to read, "I'm excited to represent all the children who have been given the gift of hearing due to their cochlear implants."

He swallowed the saliva that filled his mouth. Knew he had to sit before he lost his lunch in front of everyone. "Thank you for this honor." He stared at his own image on the back screen. Refolded the paper, glanced around the crowded room, then back to his seat without finishing the rest of the speech. Polite applause rattled through his implant.

"You look green," Lena whispered. "Turn the other way if you're going to puke."

"Uh, thank you, Noah and Lena," said Dr. Odor into the microphone. "And thank you all for coming today. Please join us for a reception and press pictures in the foyer."

Lieutenant Green was immediately on Noah's right. "Need a break? You know before you…uh."

Noah nodded and followed the lieutenant off stage.

He made it into a stall just in time.

"You okay, kid?" Lieutenant Green asked and handed Noah a bottle of water.

"Maybe," Noah said. "As long as I don't have to give another speech."

The lieutenant patted Noah on the back. "No more speeches for today. Just schmoozing among the board members."

Noah saw his death-like reflection in a mirror as he took tiny sips from the bottle. "I don't know if that's better or not. What if I can't do this? Can they fire me?"

"According to what I've been told," Lieutenant Green pressed his hand against Noah's back to guide him toward Lena and Dr. Odor, "you're the only one that can do the job. We'll figure out something."

The lieutenant's words tunneled into Noah's brain. *You're the only one. The only one.*

Lena and the doctor rushed toward them.

"Ah, there he is. Feeling better, Noah?"

"No," Noah glanced at Lena then back at the doctor. "I told you I don't do speeches."

"I can see that, now," the doctor said. "No more speeches today, but you do need to talk to people. Can you do that?"

"I don't know. Maybe."

Noah knew *maybe* was a lie.

"Lena has an idea that might help." Dr. Odor waved his hand toward a door. "Lieutenant Green, please deter anyone from entering." He shut the door and sighed. "Okay, Lena, tell him your idea."

"Can Noah really read my thoughts? I mean he told me what I had for breakfast, but maybe that was an easy guess."

This time, Noah rolled his eyes. "Sure. I just happened to pull scrambled tofu out of the air."

"Okay, well." Lena popped a bubble. "Maybe I could think the words and you could repeat them. You know, like I'm whispering in your ear."

"I don't know."

Dr. Odor clapped his hands. "Excellent problem solving, Lena. Let's try it."

"Okay, Noah, you talk first without me feeding the lines. Shake Dr. Odor's hand and say something nice."

"This is weird," Noah said.

"Just try it, you hurling geek!" Lena popped another bubble.

Noah felt smaller and smaller in comparison to Lena. He reached for Dr. Odor's hand. "Hi, uh…I'm Noah…Noah…uh Baker."

"Smooth," Lena said with a sarcastic tone. "Now, turn on the NT, listen, and repeat."

Noah touched his cochlear and pressed the NT button. Once again, he reached for Dr. Odor's hand. His brain tingled and Lena's thoughts whispered into his mind.

Good afternoon, Dr. Odor. It is a pleasure to meet you.

Noah repeated, "Good afternoon, Dr. Odor. It is a pleasure to meet you."

"Excellent!" boomed the doctor. "I knew the two of you would be a great team. Now, let's go meet and greet." He grabbed a trashcan and held it in front of Lena. She popped one more bubble then dropped the purple glob with a thump.

Noah leaned close to her as they followed the doctor out of the room. "Thanks, Lena. You know, for helping."

It felt good to think they might actually become friends.

The feeling didn't last.

"No problem." Lena flipped her hair. "Someone has to keep us from looking like idiots."

Smaller and smaller.

Chapter 18

Dr. Odor gushed praise all the way back to his office. He motioned them toward chairs in front of his desk and held out a trash can for Lena's gum that she'd been popping all the way down the hall.

"I think we can call that a success!" He clicked his pen and straightened his tie.

"Other than the speech thing."

Lena snorted.

Noah groaned.

Dr. Odor glanced at his watch then stacked the papers on his desk. "Let's not dwell on that portion of the day." He pressed a button on the desk phone. "We're ready for Captain Billings."

Noah rubbed his palms on his pant legs. Lena bit her thumb nail. Noah wondered if they were nervous about the same things. Probably not. At least he wasn't alone facing Captain Billings.

The door opened. A shadow fell across the floor followed by a tall man with a buzz haircut. Army uniform. Every button polished. Hat tucked under his arm.

"Captain Billings, welcome." Dr. Odor walked around the desk to shake the man's hand.

"Doctor. I trust all has gone well."

"Absolutely, Captain. I'd like to introduce Noah Baker and Lena Robinson, primary operatives for the DYH project."

Noah felt a strong brain tingle.

DYH stands for, Do You Hear What I Hear, Noah.

Noah leaned in close to Lena and hissed, "I know what it means."

"Just checking." Lena gave Noah a half grin.

Captain Billings glanced at each person in the room. "Is there a problem here?"

"Ha, ha, of course not," said the doctor. "Noah and Lena have some little private jokes. Don't you, kids?"

Lena punched Noah in the arm. "That's right. Lots of jokes."

Noah rubbed his arm and winced. "You bet, BUDDY. A million laughs."

"Here, Captain." The doctor pulled out his chair. "Use my desk."

The captain set his hat on the desk then leaned toward Noah and Lena. "I hope you realize the seriousness of the situation."

Noah scooted to the edge of his seat. "We understand, Captain Billings. You can count on us. Can't he, Lena?"

Lena nodded and said, "Absolutely."

He can count on one of us at least.

"Really?" Noah said and stared at Lena.

"Of course." Another half-smile that Noah was quickly recognizing as sarcasm.

"Uh, Captain Billings, I believe the children are practicing communication through the NT device." The doctor pulled his pen from his pocket and clicked it his normal three times.

"Wonderful!" Captain Billings said. He unbuttoned his jacket and leaned back in the desk chair. "I'd appreciate a demonstration."

"Certainly." Three more pen clicks. The doctor paced back and forth while rubbing his chin.

It seemed odd to Noah to see him so flustered.

"Doctor," the captain said, "is there a problem?"

The doctor didn't answer but his eyes flitted from Noah to Lena and back to Captain Billings. "Captain, if you don't mind, could you write down a series of numbers and words? There's paper in the right hand drawer. Don't let Noah see what you write."

Noah began rubbing his hands on his pant legs but stopped himself. He was sick of how Lena made him feel worthless. He leaned toward her and whispered, "Don't worry. I'll make you look good."

The quick surprise in her eyes was worth what he knew would be payback later.

Dr. Odor cleared his throat. "When Captain Billings is finished, Lena will read the words and numbers to herself and hand the paper back to him. She'll think them and Noah, you'll repeat them out loud. Captain Billings will check for accuracy. Ready?"

Noah and Lena both nodded.

The captain handed Lena the paper and stared intently at everyone like he was trying to catch them cheating.

Noah took a deep breath and waited for the tingling. The words and numbers Lena memorized rushed at him. "Gemini, 856677, Alpha, 4556321, Zebra, 87901112435, Excalibur, Lena's in charge."

Noah couldn't believe he repeated the part he was certain Lena had added herself. He huffed and turned to Lena. "You wish."

She smirked.

Captain Billings stood and leaned on the top of the desk. "That was impressive. Absolutely perfect. Except for that last part."

Dr. Odor beamed like he'd made it happen.

Captain Billings sat back in his chair. His forehead creased deep with wrinkles. His laser-eyes focused on Lena.

"Ms. Robinson," he said, "never forget, I am the one in charge."

Lena seemed to shrink into her chair and whispered, "Yes, sir."

Watching her squirm felt good and uncomfortable at the same time.

"The NT shouldn't be activated when we are in a meeting," said Captain Billings.

"Of course," Dr. Odor said, "Noah, let's shut it down for now."

"Oh, yeah. Sure." Noah reached behind his ear and pressed the button. "There. Done."

"Good," the captain said with a strong nod. "Now, it's going to take a lot of work to get you both up to speed for your first mission."

"What's the mission?" asked Lena.

"For security reasons, we can't give you all the details just yet. I can tell you you'll be making a trip to New York City."

"New York? Wow!" Lena said. "That's so cool."

"Yeah, cool." Noah added. "But it's not just for fun. Right, Captain Billings?"

Noah regretted shutting off the NT. Should have faked it. How would they punish a twelve-year-old kid who disobeyed orders? Ground him? Take away his phone?

"You'll be with other disabled children," Captain Billings said. "As a group you'll tour famous landmarks, museums, but the main focus of this team's involvement requires a visit to the United Nations. You'll need to give the impression you're having a good time, but the seriousness of the situation should be at the forefront."

Noah wasn't sure what went on at the United Nations. Knew it involved people from all over the world.

"Whose thoughts will I hear? Some king?"

Captain Billings raised his hands in front of his chest. "The details will be released to you when necessary. For now, we need to set up your training schedule. Doctor?"

"Uh…yes, Captain."

The doctor talked so fast Noah had trouble understanding all his words but got the idea.

"For security reasons, your notebooks will stay here. This is the schedule you'll follow beginning Monday." The doctor handed one sheet to each of them. "Your parents are receiving a packet of information inviting you to a three-day camp for disabled children. The truth is you'll be in a secure government location receiving mission training."

Lena interrupted, "So, we're supposed to lie to our parents?" She sounded a little desperate. "I'm terrible at that."

"You'll be fine," said Dr. Odor.

Lena stood. "That's what you said about Noah's speech. Remember his hurling performance?"

Noah cringed. She wasn't ever going to let him forget that humiliation.

Captain Billings left the desk to stand in front of the courtyard window. "Lena, are you familiar with the Revolutionary War?"

"Yes, sir." She fell back in her chair like her legs had grown weak. "We fought for independence from England. I remember everything I've ever heard or read about it."

The captain's words bounced off the window glass. "Have you read about a woman named, Lydia Barrington Darragh?"

"No, sir."

Noah noticed Lena's forehead wrinkle. He was certain *not knowing* was not acceptable to her. He watched as she tapped the heel of her good leg on the floor. As hateful as she'd been, he felt a need to help her.

Knew she'd resent it if he did.

"Lydia Barrington Darragh was the mother of a patriot soldier. Lydia and her husband were against violence. But Lydia found a way to help her country and her son by spying on the British soldiers quartered in her home during the British occupation. When she brought food to the officers, she listened to their plans. She hid messages under cloth covered buttons on her younger son's clothing.

Lydia sent the boy to meet his brother who was serving in General George Washington's Continental Army. Those messages saved the patriots from countless lost battles because they were forewarned."

Captain Billings turned and sat on the desk edge in front of Lena. "Lydia didn't lie, she just didn't let the British soldiers know she was remembering what they said. Think you could have that kind of courage?"

"Maybe," said Lena. "But that doesn't help me tell my parents a bunch of lies they'll figure out. They're really smart."

Dr. Odor stepped forward and said, "You will be going to a camp." He glanced toward the captain like he was uneasy about interrupting. "It will be in a secure location instead of by a lake with canoes. You'll be with children who have disabilities, but there will only be two of you."

Captain Billings stood and sifted through some papers. He handed Lena a picture of a shirt with an owl logo on it. "We'll even make you camp t-shirts to make it believable."

Noah had been silent but felt a need to convince her. "We can do this, Lena." He put his hand on her shoulder. "As long as I don't have to give a speech."

She smiled at him.

A genuine smile.

Just for a second, Noah thought he might have seen a small piece of the real Lena.

Chapter 19

At home that night, Noah went to bed early and tried to force sleep. His brain refused to shut off the first day of training—the speech, the captain's intense stare, and Lena's smile. The one that gave him a hint she was a scared kid, just like him.

The bedroom door creaked open. Tod's shape hesitated with faint light behind him. The clock read 11:55 PM. Noah reached for his cochlear and snapped it into place.

"You just barely made curfew," Noah said.

"Plenty of time. Why do you care?"

Noah ignored Tod's attitude. "I couldn't sleep."

He reached behind his ear and activated the NT button. Wanted real thoughts, not just insults.

A robotic curse surged through Noah's cochlear when Tod stubbed his toe.

Coach will freak if I hurt that ankle again.

"How's your ankle you hurt at the game?" Noah asked.

Tod hissed. More curses. "Still hurts! How'd you know? You weren't there."

Noah heard disappointment in his words. He'd gotten out of the habit of going to Tod's games since he couldn't hear. Didn't think Tod even noticed.

"I heard Mom and Dad talk about it."

"No big deal," Tod said.

Noah heard his brother's bed squeak then a big sigh. Silence.

"Tod," Noah said after a few seconds, "does anything ever scare you?"

Noah pulled back the sheet and swung his legs over the edge of his bed. "You know. Have you ever been afraid of something?"

You mean like when I thought I killed you?

Woah! Noah felt like someone punched him in the gut. All he remembered about the accident was getting Tod's phone from the floor of the backseat. Nobody told him Tod thought he'd killed his little brother.

Maybe Tod never told anyone.

"Everybody's afraid of something," Tod said. "You freaked about that lame camp?"

"A little." Noah sat cross-legged on his bed. "I'm terrible at this Ambassador stuff. I had to make a speech today!"

"Ha, that's bad." Tod kicked off one shoe. "You hurl all over the people on the front row?"

"Almost," Noah said.

He groaned and grabbed his head with his hands. "I don't know why they chose me."

"Not that I care, little brother, but they must think you have the guts to do it or they'd get another kid." Noah heard a robotic thud as Tod's other shoe dropped. "Now, shut up and go to sleep."

Noah ached to tell the real reason he couldn't sleep. That he wasn't going to a normal camp. That the government couldn't give the job to someone else. He wanted to warn his brother about the bad people.

Noah flopped to his back knowing he couldn't tell Tod any of it. Not safe.

He reached to pull off the cochlear.

Stopped himself. There was one thing he could say to Tod. Something he should have said a long time ago. He pulled in a deep breath.

"It wasn't your fault, Tod." The words were out before he had time to quiet them. "The accident. Me going deaf wasn't your fault. It just happened."

Silence.

"Tod?" Noah sat up and pulled his knees to his chest. "Did you hear me? Nobody blames you."

I blame me. It will always be my fault.

Noah ducked when he saw the shadow of some object flying across the room.

"Go to sleep!"

Noah pulled off the cochlear and flopped back and forth on his bed. He was frustrated Tod wouldn't talk and that his brother's thoughts only gave Noah more to keep him awake. He settled on his back and stared at glowing stars some other kid left on the ceiling. Seven big. Seven small. He counted them over and over.

Long after Tod was snoring, Noah slipped into disturbing dreams of being forced to give a speech at the United Nations.

And running from a black SUV in a parking garage.

Chapter 20

…0800 hours…

Mom was at work. Dad was mowing lawns. Tod was asleep. Noah waited on the front porch, his sleeping bag and backpack stacked beside him. He'd worked his way through being scared in the night to being determined.

"…they must think you have the guts to do it, or they'd get another kid."

Noah wanted to prove to his brother he could do more than just fool people. Even if he couldn't tell him the classified information about the camp and the mission.

A long government car pulled into the driveway. Lieutenant Green opened the door and waved.

"Ready?" He called as he opened the trunk.

Noah gave him a thumbs up and jogged to the car. He leaned into the backseat. Waited to smell grape. Wasn't disappointed.

Three pops, then, "If it isn't Upchuck!" Three more pops. "Corporal Powell and I have a bet."

"What kind of bet?" Noah asked as he crawled onto the seat beside Lena.

"How long before you hurl again." Lena blew a huge bubble. She picked it from her mouth and held it with two fingers to admire it.

"I say any minute." She deflated the bubble and stuck it into her mouth. "That's why Dr. Odor sent you this really cool puke bucket."

She held up a plastic container.

"Very funny, Bubbles. I'd like to take a bet on how long before he makes you throw away that gum. Permanently. Maybe that's what the bucket is really for."

Lena did a typical eye roll and turned to face the window.

Noah tapped her on the shoulder. "Hey, I thought you said you didn't lie."

She turned and faced him. The color of her eyes still indescribable to him.

"Oh, I have no problem lying to you. I just have a hard time lying to my parents." Two bubble pops. "They can always tell."

Noah glanced at the front seat. Corporal Powell grinned as she turned to check traffic before pulling onto the main road. The lieutenant winked through the visor mirror.

Lena turned in the seat and whispered, "Is the NT off? I don't like the idea of you being inside my head."

"Got something to hide, Lena?" Noah laughed, but stopped when he saw the anger in her eyes. "Yes, it's off. Dr. Odor said not to leave it on all the time. Just when I need it."

"Okay, kids. First, I need your cell phones. Security is pretty tight where we're going." He turned in the seat and held out his hand.

"But I need my phone!" Lena said.

Lieutenant Green raised his eyebrows. He snapped his fingers twice and reached a flat palm toward her.

Lena groaned and slapped her purple phone onto his hand.

"What about our parents?" Noah asked. "Won't they ask questions if they don't hear from us?"

"It's all covered. Phone, please." Another finger snap. He took Noah's phone and turned to face front. "The drive will take us approximately one hour. Dr. Odor sent your notebooks for you to work on the acronym section."

He squared himself in his seat and adjusted his sunglasses. "We'll close the privacy-window, so our conversations won't distract you."

He pushed a button on the dash and thick glass raised to section off the back seat.

"I guess we better study." Noah reached for the notebook with his name.

"You study," Lena said. "I'll read through it then enjoy the ride."

She opened her notebook.

Noah watched her fingers run down the columns of acronyms and explanations. She was like a machine scanning the words and letters. He opened his own notebook. He had sort of learned the first page when Lena slammed her notebook shut. She set it aside, rested her head against the seat, and closed her eyes.

"Crazy," he said to himself. How am I supposed to compete with that?

"…must have fooled them…"

Maybe Tod was right. Noah felt like a fake.

He peered through the window as the car sped past homes and businesses. They merged onto 29-N. Why hadn't he asked where they were going?

"…camp will be in a secure location…"

Even more questions crowded his thoughts when a second set of dark windows blocked their view of the traffic beside them. Lena pulled one side of her earphones from her head.

Lieutenant Green's voice spoke through the car's speakers, "For your own safety, Captain Billings instructed us to hide our destination from you. You'll go dark until we arrive."

Several pops came from inside Lena's mouth. "For our safety?"

"Yeah." Noah scrubbed his hands on the legs of his shorts. "Didn't Dr. Odor tell you about the bad people?"

Lena's eyes went wide. "Sure! But I thought he was just trying to scare me into keeping my mouth shut. I didn't think he was serious."

More pops.

"I thought the same. Until I saw the black SUV."

"What SUV?"

"The one that's been following my family. I forgot to look for it this morning."

"That's creepy. Why didn't you tell me?"

"We didn't even meet until Saturday. There wasn't a lot of time to share our secrets. Besides, it's probably just the government's way of keeping us safe. They may be tailing your family too."

Lena threw her hands up in the air and turned toward the door. "Why are we doing this, Noah?"

Lena's words bounced off the window she couldn't even look through.

"Don't know about you, but I want to help my family. Medical stuff. Pay for college," he said.

"Sure, that's why I'm doing it. A little for myself too. They promised me this bionic leg." She tapped her leg. "They said I'd be able to run again."

Noah wanted to ask how she lost her leg. Stopped himself several times until he slammed the notebook shut and whispered, "How did it happen, Lena? Tell me about your leg."

She stiffened. "Don't go there, Upchuck. Not ever."

She pulled the hood of her sweatshirt over her head and curled into the seat.

Noah opened his notebook again and tried to ignore the complicated girl sleeping in the seat beside him. He lost track of time until he felt the car brake and make a sharp turn. He snapped his head to the right when the dark window whirred down. All he could see on his side of the car was pine trees. For miles. The car turned several curves, slowed even more. Stopped.

"Wow!" he said.

"Double wow!"

Noah turned toward Lena's voice. She wasn't reacting to miles of trees. She was staring at their "camp."

Chapter 21

It looked more like a compound.

Trucks. Long buildings.

Lots of adults. Some military. Some in dark clothes. Sunglasses.

A guard tower?

The car door opened.

"Welcome to Camp Alpha!" Lieutenant Green said. "Everybody out."

Noah squinted in the bright sun. Pine tree smells mingled with the scent of grape gum. He turned and stared at Lena.

"Do you have to chew that stuff all the time?"

Pop! Pop! Pop!

"Yes, I do," Lena said. "Do you have to..."

"Okay, remember you two are a team." Lieutenant Green turned to the driver. "Corporal Powell, after you park the car, meet us in the captain's office."

She saluted. "Yes, sir."

Noah shook out his fingers before he picked up his gear. The secret location stuff bugged him. It had to be driving Lena crazy.

"Where are we?" he whispered close to her ear.

"Not sure." Lena pivoted in a circle as they walked. "Wooded area, highly guarded, west of Baltimore. That makes it northwest of DC. I have a theory, but not ready to commit."

Noah snorted. "That's because you don't know."

"And I suppose you do." She flipped her hair into his face and jogged ahead.

Lieutenant Green turned. "You coming, Noah?"

"Yes sir!" Noah adjusted his backpack and ran to catch up.

"Whoever figures out where we are first wins," he said to Lena.

"Great idea. Winner will be in charge." She blew a bubble. "You know how I like being in charge."

"Ha!" he said. "Tell that to Captain Billings."

The lieutenant led them into a tan concrete block building. The smell of new paint and wood shavings replaced the pine outside.

A part of Noah wanted it to be more camp-like. He knew they were there to train for a mission, but canoes and a rope swing over a lake would have been cool. He tried to remember what the audiologist said about swimming with a cochlear.

Lieutenant Green motioned for them to sit on the only pieces of furniture in a waiting room. A deep robotic voice answered the lieutenant's knock.

Noah couldn't understand the muffled words.

"This place is brand-new," said Lena.

"No kidding. I bet the paint is still wet on the walls." Noah reached a finger to test the dryness when the lieutenant stepped back into the room.

"Leave your gear here and follow me," Lieutenant Green said.

Lena's signature gum pops echoed off the walls. The lieutenant held a trashcan in front of her. "No gum in this office. Ever."

One more bubble pop then Lena dropped the juicy blob into the trash.

"Yes, sir," she said and gave a sarcastic salute.

Lieutenant Green had become more serious since they got in the car that morning. Noah missed the guy who cracked jokes and stole bacon from his breakfast tray.

"DYH reporting, Captain Billings," the lieutenant said and held a salute.

The captain continued writing, then stared over the top of his reading glasses. After a few seconds, he returned the lieutenant's salute.

"Welcome, team." He waved his hand toward chairs in front of his desk. "Please be seated."

Noah took a deep breath and silently begged his stomach to stop rolling. Lena's lip biting confirmed her stress. Probably wishing for a piece of gum.

The room had a fresh coat of light blue paint. A large roll of carpet rested against the wall and unpacked boxes were stacked in the corner. It was like the building and its contents had been put together in a hurry.

Just for them.

The captain pulled a handkerchief from his pocket and blew his nose, honking like a robotic goose. "Pine trees," he mumbled. "Okay, let's get down to business."

He folded the handkerchief in a perfect square and put it in his hip pocket. "Lieutenant Green, I assume you confiscated their phones."

"Yes, sir," the lieutenant said. "The tracking settings have already been set up for the arranged location."

"What arranged location?" Noah asked. "I thought this is the camp."

"This is your training location, but for your protection, we have to convince your family and others that you are at Camp Wahuhi in Virginia. Our tech people will instruct you on the plan when we finish here.

"What's *wahuhi* mean?" Lena asked.

"It means *owl* in Cherokee, but that's not important," said the captain. "Hold your questions until later."

Lena stared at Noah. She raised her eyebrows and scratched her ear. Noah knew she was trying to tell him something, but he didn't have a clue. A knock sounded at the door.

"Oh, good. Here's Corporal Powell," said Captain Billings. "We can get you settled in your quarters and start on your schedules."

While the adults were distracted, Lena leaned in and whispered something. She wasn't on Noah's cochlear side, so he just shook his head.

Everyone stood. "Noah, you will go with Lieutenant Green and Lena with Corporal Powell. They will be your chaperones. If you have any issues or questions, ask them." He put his glasses on and picked up the same papers he was reading earlier. When they didn't leave, he looked up and said, "Dismissed."

"Let's go, team," Lieutenant Green said. "Grab your gear." He led them from the building and across the compound. Another set of trucks roared past them stirring dust and crushing pine cones.

Noah was amazed at the sounds he heard through his cochlear. The caw from a black bird flying overhead. The pushunk, pushunk of a nail gun on a roof behind them. He sometimes wondered if he was truly hearing or just remembering from the past.

Lena tapped him on the shoulder. "I was trying to tell you..."

The whumpa-whumpa-whumpa of a low flying helicopter drowned out her words. Before they could look up, Lieutenant Green rushed them through a door. Inside the building, the helicopter engine and propeller were muffled, but still loud enough to know it was big. Bigger than anything Noah had ever seen up close.

"Noah!" Lena hissed. "We've got to talk."

"Okay," he said. "Just get on the side where my cochlear is. Easier to hear."

"No time to talk now," the lieutenant inserted over his shoulder. He turned to face them. "Lena, you will be in Room C with Corporal Powell in the adjoining room." He waved her through the door. "Noah, you are in Room A and I'll be next door." He opened door A and followed Noah into the room.

Again, fresh paint, polished concrete floor, very plain. The room had a twin bed and several pieces of simple furniture. A blank bulletin board was fastened to the wall. There were three doors. One was open to a bathroom with a shower. The second a closet with metal hangers and a fire extinguisher. Lieutenant Green unbolted the third door and opened it.

"This goes to my quarters. It can only be opened from your side." He pointed to a red button just under the lip of the nightstand. "Here's your panic button. You'll probably never need it, but if you push it, half the military will come to your rescue. I strongly encourage you not to push it for a joke."

He cleared his throat and looked Noah straight in the eye. "If you haven't noticed, Captain Billings doesn't have a sense of humor."

"I noticed." Noah pivoted in a circle. "Where's the TV?"

"Ha!" The lieutenant laughed, then covered his mouth with his hand. "Your schedule won't have much free time, but if you want to watch TV, there's a rec room at the other end of the hall." His steps echoed throughout the space when he headed toward the exit. "You and Lena have a meeting in the rec room with the tech crew at eleven hundred. That's in ten minutes. Time enough to stow your gear and change into this really cool camp t-shirt."

He tossed a booger green colored shirt to Noah.

"Could they find something any uglier?" Noah said. He held it up to read the brown logo with a cartoon-like owl.

The lieutenant gave him a quick smile. "I'll let Captain Billings know your request."

And then he was gone.

Noah threw the shirt on the one chair in the room. He walked to the window and watched a squirrel race across the road in front of a big camouflaged truck. He puzzled over the last two weeks. How had he gone from just wanting to hear, to a military compound in the middle of who knows where? He shook himself from his thoughts and rolled out his sleeping bag.

When he dumped his underwear and stuff into a drawer, he found a note his mom had slipped between his clothes. He ached for his family in a way that surprised him. He even wished Tod could be in a bed across the room, pelting shoes and dirty socks. Noah breathed in a deep breath of paint fumes. Imagined Tod making fun of him from the sidelines while he did boot camp pushups and obstacle courses.

What did any of this have to do with reading minds?

Chapter 22

The tech guy, everyone called Einstein, hunched over a laptop while Noah and Lena waited for his next instructions. They'd posed in front of a green screen for over an hour. Lena had convinced Einstein it wouldn't be believable without her gum.

"Noah, let's try a thumbs up," Einstein said. "Lena, act like you have your right arm around the person beside you."

"I would never do that," Lena muttered.

She did what he said anyway.

"Okay, great!" Einstein said. "Now, big smiles. Make your parents think you're having the time of your lives."

"Oh, we are, aren't we, Lena?" Noah asked.

He heard Lena's laugh beside him.

"That's perfect." Einstein tapped his laptop keys like his fingers were in a race.

Noah studied the tech's face. Not military. Seemed really young to be so smart. He wondered what Captain Billings had used to get him to work for them.

"That's the last shot," Einstein said. "Why don't you two get something to drink from the fridge while I do my magic on these pics."

Noah groaned and stretched the muscles in his back. He followed Lena as they stepped over cables on the floor. Lena got to the kitchen first and grabbed a water from the small fridge. She sat down and began taking sips from the bottle.

"Nothing for me?" Noah asked.

"Not your waitress, Upchuck," she said, then took a longer drink.

He pulled on the door, hoping for more than water. "Perfect!" He grabbed a Pepsi and guzzled half of it. "Burrrrppppp!"

"Seriously! Could you be more disgusting?" Lena turned her chair around so her back was to him.

"I'll work on it, Bubbles, but my schedule is pretty full."

"Are you two still bickering?" Neither of them noticed Lieutenant Green entering the room.

He leaned over the tech's shoulder. "That's incredible, Einstein. Did you get the group shot?"

Einstein's fingers flew across the keys.

"Outstanding! The captain will be pleased. Can you show it on the wall TV?" He didn't wait for an answer, but lined chairs in front of the screen. "You two, sit."

Noah chugged the rest of his drink and tossed the can in the recycle bin. Just as he sat beside Lena, the screen lit up with a picture of him playing catch with some guys he'd never seen before. Then there was a picture of Lena playing tether ball, a shot of the Camp Wahuhi Wilderness sign, and both of them roasting hot dogs by a campfire. Pictures scrolled on the screen of kids in canoes on a lake, Noah stuffing marshmallows in his mouth, and Lena in front of a cabin with some other girls. The final shot was one of those large group staged shots. Everyone had on the hideous Camp Wahuhi shirts like the ones Lena and Noah were wearing. The two of them were mixed in with the other kids like they were all best friends.

"How did you do that?" Lena asked.

Einstein polished his nails on his shirt and blew on them. "Just one of my many skills."

"Okay, show's over," Lieutenant Green said. "These pictures will be loaded onto your cell phones and sent to your parents throughout the next three days." He handed Noah and Lena two postcards each. "You have fifteen minutes to write some bogus postcards for your parents. Lunch after that then your real training begins."

"What are we supposed to write?" Noah asked.

"Make it vague," Lieutenant Green said. "Here are some suggestions. Put it in your own words though. Convince them."

He handed them sheets of paper with 'Having a great time' kind of messages. "Don't forget the address. We could make labels, but it needs to be in your own handwriting."

Noah took the cards and wondered what it would be like to send post cards from a real camp. Remembered the camp his parents were planning to send him to before the accident. Like a normal kid, doing normal things.

Always before and after.

Noah glanced at Lena. Her eyebrows were wrinkled like she was in pain. He knew it bothered her to lie to her parents.

Shouldn't it bother him more?

Chapter 23

After lunch, the lieutenant walked them from the mess hall to the building where their rooms were.

"Okay, team," he said louder than necessary. "Captain Billings isn't ready for you yet, so the rec room is yours."

He spread his arms wide and smiled.

"Can we have our phones back?" Lena asked.

"Nope," he tossed over his shoulder as he left.

"So what do we do now?" Lena stomped her foot.

Noah pictured her as a little girl having a lower lip temper tantrum. A smile spread across his face. He erased it before she noticed.

"A recreation room should have something fun hidden somewhere," he said. The corner cabinet's doors squeaked when he opened them. The mustiness didn't fit with the new construction smells in the building.

"Puzzles?" he asked.

"Seriously? What are we, kindergarteners?" She pulled a piece of gum from her pocket.

"Okay. How about checkers?" Noah turned to show Lena a ragged box of checkers with the board missing.

That's when a green table against the wall caught his eye. He rummaged through the cabinet some more and held up a small white ball.

"Ping Pong?"

"Sure. I've played a few times," she said, a bored tone in her voice.

Noah found two paddles, one ball, and the net. After the third game of Noah getting skunked, he slammed down his paddle.

"Is there anything you *can't* do?" Sweat burned his eyes and ran between his shoulder blades.

Lena wasn't even breathing hard.

Lena shrugged her shoulders. "I'm not that good," she said and took a long drink from her water. "You're just that bad."

Noah started to protest. Opened his mouth to tell her it was only the second time he'd ever played, when Lena turned and pointed at him. "I forgot to tell you what I was trying to say earlier. I wanted to tell you…"

"Hold on." Noah grabbed her arm. "Can you show me how to turn on the water? It's kinda tricky."

He pulled her toward the bathroom.

"What?" Lena yanked her arm from his fingers. "That's just weird."

"Trust me," he whispered in her ear.

They squeezed into the room and Noah attempted to turn the faucet. "See, I can't get this to work."

"What an idiot!" She stepped in front of him and gave the handle a twist. "It works fine. You just, you know, TURN it."

"Oh, I see now. Thanks."

He blocked her way to leave and started talking while he washed his hands. "Probably worrying about nothing, but I was wondering if someone is listening when we're alone. Maybe even cameras."

He fiddled with the soap dispenser longer than necessary and kept talking. "Water should block our words and I don't think they would have a camera in here. You know, a bathroom."

Lena nodded. "Not bad, Upchuck. I guess you aren't totally hopeless."

"Talk fast," Noah muttered, "I can only wash my hands so long."

"Okay. I was trying to tell you to turn on the NT, so we could tell what the captain was thinking."

"Oh, that would have been good," Noah said. "Maybe we need a signal."

Lena snapped her fingers. "Good! I'll pull on my ear. Don't let anyone know what you're doing when you turn it on though."

Noah rolled his eyes and said, "Oh, thanks for the tip."

He turned off the faucet and grabbed a paper towel. They had just walked back to the ping pong table when Lieutenant Green's voice boomed from the doorway.

"Free time is over. Captain Billings is ready." He turned, and they followed him to an elevator. The lieutenant pulled a key from his belt and pushed it into a slot while pressing an unmarked button. When the doors closed, the elevator dropped. Floor after floor after floor.

"What is this? A bomb shelter?" Noah asked.

"Something like that," Lieutenant Green said.

Noah and Lena turned to each other with wide eyes.

The doors slid open and they entered a stark white room divided into glass paneled cubicles. A mix of civilian and military people sat in front of computer monitors. Their attention only on the words and numbers in front of them.

"Keep your eyes straight ahead and stay behind me," said the lieutenant.

"What did he say?" Noah asked Lena.

She used both hands to gesture eyes front. "Just follow me."

"You're not in charge yet," Noah mumbled.

"That's what you think," she said.

They trailed Lieutenant Green up some open metal stairs. Robotic pings sounded through Noah's cochlear with each footstep.

"This way, team," said Lieutenant Green. He held the door open to a glass walled office. As Lena passed by him, the lieutenant produced a trash can.

Captain Billings sat at a simple desk. His attention focused on the file in front of him. Not on the line of people filing through the door.

"Team DYH reporting for training," said the lieutenant.

Captain Billings stared over the top of his glasses. No smile, no words, just two caterpillar eyebrows bouncing above the dark frames. He cleared his throat and leaned back in his chair. Lots of staring first at Noah and then Lena. He motioned for them to sit. Still no words.

Noah squirmed in his seat. He glanced at Lena when she reached in her pocket for gum then sat on her hands instead. They both jumped when the captain's voice boomed across the desk.

"What you are about to learn is top secret." More silence and caterpillar movement above his glasses. "A critical meeting will be occurring in the next couple weeks at the United Nations. It has been discovered that several U.S. citizens are missing in the small country of Viracocha. We believe rebels have kidnapped them in hopes the United States will get involved in the civil war in their country. Our undercover intel has told us Viracocha's Ambassador to the United Nations supports the rebels and the holding of these prisoners."

Captain Billings walked around the desk and sat on the edge. "We need more specific information of the ambassador's involvement and the location of the hostages."

He gave an intense stare at Noah and grabbed two notebooks from the side of his desk. "Noah, that's where your ability will be imperative."

Noah reached for the notebook the captain passed to him. He pushed down the groan building in his throat. There had to be a hundred pages. Maybe more. He glanced at Lena who was already flipping through the first section. Probably memorizing as she scanned.

"These notebooks contain your schedules for the rest of the week. When you aren't training, you should be studying the information about Viracocha, the United Nations building, and a crash course in the Spanish language."

"Why Spanish?" asked Noah.

"Duh, Noah. The representative speaks Spanish." Lena rolled her eyes.

"Duh, Lena. How do we know he doesn't think in English?" Noah folded his arms across his chest.

Captain Billings stared intently at Lieutenant Green. "Do they understand the seriousness of this mission?"

"They do. They will."

Chapter 24

"**R**epeat what you heard," said the technician.

Same instructions Noah had heard for the last hour. He stopped counting how many times after ten. He waited for the brain tingle and repeated, "Roses, popcorn, Empire something."

"Good," said the tech, "but it was Empire State Building."

She tapped her fingers on the side of her clipboard and scribbled more notes.

They'd started in a soundproof room with two chairs side-by-side. The tech began with random words that were easy for Noah to retrieve from her thoughts and repeat. After every few words, she moved her chair a few feet away from his. Her actual words, through his cochlear, sounded robotic like everyone else's. Her thought words were different. They were clear and there was an accent there he couldn't identify.

"Okay, now I'm going to move to the next room." She stood and opened the door. "Just repeat whatever words you hear."

Noah was learning to anticipate the thoughts with the tingling in his brain, but also a sense of words that weren't his. "This is getting old fast," he said.

Robotic words came over the speaker in the corner next to the ceiling. "I know it is tedious, but it's important to your training."

"Those were your thoughts, not mine," said Noah. "You think this is getting old fast."

There was a pause while he assumed she was writing notes.

Noah jumped when the door opened. "Good work, Noah. Let's take a break. There's a restroom and water fountain on the left in the hall."

He stayed in the restroom longer than he needed, just to have some time away from the tech. The accent was bugging him. He wished Lena could hear it. She'd know what language the tech spoke when it wasn't English. He rolled his shoulders to loosen the tight muscles. Considered doing some pushups on the floor. He looked at the concrete under his feet and used the wall instead. After his arms began to ache, he met the tech in the hall.

"Are you not feeling well?" asked the tech.

"I'm fine," Noah said and felt his face burn.

"Good. Follow me." She held the clipboard against her chest and walked down the hall.

Noah followed her into what looked like a break room. He felt the beat of music and the ting of notes. Conversations mingled with the sound of ice ricocheting off the sides of cups at the dispenser. He was getting used to the eecks and beeps of sound through the cochlear but hadn't been around this much noise since it was activated. Everything seemed magnified as it bounced off the cinder block walls. It was on the edge of being overwhelming.

"Have a seat, Noah. Do you want a soft drink?" She didn't wait for an answer but headed to the counter.

It seemed odd that everyone in the room ignored him. Did a kid show up every day in their underground break room?

"Here you go." She set a frosty cup in front of him and sat in the chair across the table. "Let's continue."

"We're working here?" Noah asked.

"Absolutely. We need to know how your ability is affected by additional stimuli." She clicked her pen and stared at the clipboard in her hands. "What do you hear?"

Noah waited for the tingle, tried to ignore the laughter and scraping chairs. "Hmm…windmill, uh…"

"That's correct, but there's more. Concentrate."

Noah closed his eyes. He ignored the noisy room. "Windmill, black…uh…black car, Wall Street."

"Excellent!" The tech scribbled notes. "Let's move to a table with some other people." She stood and led him to the center of the room. "May we join you?" The two guys dressed in camouflage uniforms nodded. She motioned toward the chair for Noah. "This will be the last test for today. Concentrate."

Noah realized these people had to be part of the test. It was a simulation. "Cool," he said quietly.

"Excuse me," the tech said.

"Oh, nothing." Noah squirmed in his seat and leaned forward. "I'm ready."

"You can do this, Noah. Just concentrate." She hesitated. The two men at the table began talking, as did everyone around them.

Noah closed his eyes and listened with his mind. He fought to ignore the hum of voices as well as countless thoughts. He rubbed his clammy palms on the legs of his shorts.

"Just relax. Try to picture the words."

Finally, it was like the tech's words floated to the top. He could see them. They were red.

"I've got it! October 25, uh, Italy, and some numbers."

"Focus on the numbers. What are the numbers?" The tech's robotic words sounded distant.

Noah struggled again to push everything else away. "Got it!" he said. "31, 28, 25987."

His eyes snapped open. "Is that right?"

The tech grinned. "Perfect!"

The two guys at the table gave him a thumbs up.

"Just remember those numbers." She narrowed her eyes and said, "What do you hear now?"

Noah was proud he was able to separate her thoughts from everyone else's. Her words were clear as could be, but he hesitated. "I'm not sure." He wanted this to be over, but the thoughts he was hearing were bizarre compared to her others.

"How about now?" the woman asked.

Noah coughed and said, "I don't think I can say that to you."

"I need you to concentrate. What did you hear?"

"Okay. You think you look fat in those pants."

"What?!" She stood up and looked in the wall mirror across the room.

Noah saw the two guys trying to cover their laughter. One filled his mouth with fries. The other checked his phone.

"Not my words," Noah said. "You thought it."

The tech grabbed her clipboard and stood. "We're finished for today. Return to Captain Billings's office."

Noah stared at the table after the tech left. He made finger circles in the sweat from his drink. He pictured himself using the cochlear at school. Might be fun to know what people really thought. Other kids. Teachers. Maybe listen to answers from a smart kid's mind and ace every test.

Could he really do that?

Nah. He was kind of lazy about schoolwork, but he was never a cheater.

He followed everyone as they left the break room. It took him a bit to navigate his way back to Captain Billings's office. The door was open.

"Yes, he's making progress, but I'm not sure about the long-term… of the…"

The tech's squeaky cochlear words cut in and out. Noah wanted to hear more but decided to let them know he was there.

"Excuse me," Noah said as he tapped his knuckles on the door.

Captain Billings stared over the top of his glasses. The tech jumped to her feet. Her face flushed red.

"Welcome, Noah," said the captain. "Have a seat."

Noah pressed his lips together and slumped into an empty chair in front of the desk.

The tech squirmed in her seat and began. "Noah, I was just giving Captain Billings a report on your neurological transmissions training."

She glanced at the captain.

He nodded.

"First," the tech said, "I need you to remove your cochlear processor."

She held a glass container in her open palm.

He removed it and wondered why she didn't just ask him to shut it off. Maybe she didn't trust him. The silence was immediate. His palms began to sweat.

The tech pointed to her lips and said, "Now, please repeat the numbers you retrieved from my thoughts while we were in the break room."

Noah sat up straight in his chair. "What did you say?"

The captain answered for the tech with exaggerated words. "Repeat the numbers."

Noah scrubbed his palms again. "The ones from the break room? Okay." He closed his eyes and tried picturing like the tech had suggested. "Uh…28, 13, and…"

He was blank. "All I can remember is the first and last of the long list. 2 and 7."

Noah glanced from one to the other.

Captain Billings raised his eyebrows toward the tech.

The tech gave a slight shake of her head and handed Noah's cochlear to him.

Noah reconnected it. He winced with the squeaks and beeps.

The captain stood. "Thank you, Noah. That's all for now. Go to your quarters to change into work-out clothes, then report to the track."

Noah hesitated.

"Dismissed."

"Yes, sir."

Curiosity wormed inside him as he stepped from the room. The door closed but the tech's thoughts still entered his brain.

He totally messed up those numbers. Looks like we go to PLAN B.

Noah startled when a door slammed. He glanced toward the people working at their desks below him then tripped down the stairs.

* * * * * *

After a quick change of clothes in his quarters, Noah dropped onto the metal bench beside the running track. He shaded his eyes to watch a runner jogging on the far side of the track. Just as the runner rounded the south end, the jog became a sprint.

"She's fast isn't she?" Lieutenant Green said behind him.

The lieutenant planted his foot on the bench and did some stretches.

"Really fast," Noah said. "Who is she?"

"You're kidding, right?"

"No, why?" Noah stood with his hand on his hips.

Lieutenant Green stopped stretching. "That's your partner."

"What did you say?" Noah asked.

"It's Lena. Looks like that blade runner leg is working just fine," said Lieutenant Green.

Lena trotted toward them. Her gait was different. Noah tried not to stare but couldn't help it. It was the first time he'd seen her in anything but long pants. First time he knew where her real leg ended and her artificial one began. There was a curved metal blade attached to her leg stump. He remembered seeing something like it on the news.

Pure joy shone on her face.

She grabbed a water bottle from the bench and chugged it. "What were you talking about?"

"You!" Noah said. "Man, you are fast!"

Noah was surprised to see Lena blush.

"Well, not up to my time from before…before, you know." She stared into the distance. "I'll get there."

She looked back to Noah. "What about you? You wanna race?"

Noah choked on a breath. "Uh, no. I'll pass. Wouldn't want to destroy your record. You know. Not just yet."

"You sure?" Lena made her voice lilt in a sarcastic tone.

Noah held up his thumb.

"Okay, then I'm going to the pool to check out my swim leg." She threw her towel over her shoulder. "See you at supper, Upchuck."

Noah saw a bubble form and pop in her mouth, but the sound was swallowed up in the wind. Lena tossed her hair and jogged away.

"Hey," said Lieutenant Green, "you really that fast?"

Noah rolled his eyes. "Uh, no." He hesitated and faced the lieutenant. "I'm not about to admit that to her though."

The lieutenant sat and motioned for Noah to join him. "You need to listen to me kid. This mission stuff is a big deal. A lot of people will be counting on you."

He leaned his elbows on his knees. "If you can't do something, or you notice something, you better be honest. It could be a matter of life and death for you and your team."

Noah was silent.

"Did you hear me, Noah?" Lieutenant Green asked.

"Got it," said Noah.

They both stood. "Okay, let's go see what kind of runner you are."

Noah jogged onto the track. As he fell further and further behind the lieutenant, Noah puzzled over the thoughts he'd heard outside the captain's office.

Messed up the numbers.

PLAN B.

What is Plan B and how many more goofs before they decide to fire him?

Chapter 25

Noah and Lena waited outside the captain's office after an intense morning of self-defense classes. With each move and counter move they'd been taught, Noah's muscles had grown tighter. Of course, Lena was better at most of it. Everything except when it involved upper body strength. His pushups had worked well for him there. Noah knew better than to tease her about it though.

Voices from the captain's office hissed through Noah's cochlear. He wiped his palms on his jeans until he thought he might rub blisters. Lena, of course, blew bubble after bubble.

"What do you think they're planning now?" asked Noah.

Pop! Pop!

"No idea. Did you try reading their thoughts?" Lena asked.

She gave him a hopeful look.

"Of course." Noah felt heat travel up his neck as soon as the lie left his lips. He scratched his head and pressed the switch on his processor. Hoped Lena hadn't noticed.

The door opened and they both jumped.

Lieutenant Green held a trash can for Lena's gum, then motioned them into the office.

They filed through the door and sat again in chairs facing Captain Billings. He ignored them until he picked up the papers he had been reading and tapped them together on the desk.

"Well, Noah and Lena, I've just finished reviewing the reports on your training. You have both made tremendous progress, but we need to add another element to the plan."

"You mean, Plan B," Noah said before he could stop himself. He saw Lena's reaction from the side of his vision.

"What's Plan B?" she asked. "And why do you know about it and I don't?"

The captain shot a stinging look at Lieutenant Green. "Lieutenant, would you like to enlighten me about why Noah would have that kind of information?"

The lieutenant looked stunned and held up his open palms.

"It's not his fault, Captain Billings," Noah said and then sighed. "I heard the tech's thoughts after I left your office today."

Captain Billings turned again to Lieutenant Green. "We need to have some way to control when Noah can use his NT."

"Absolutely," said the lieutenant. "I'll contact Dr. Odor about that. For now, Noah, shut it off when you're in this office."

Noah nodded and reached for the button on his cochlear. "Off."

He shrugged at Lena.

"Now, down to business," said Captain Billings. "We are running out of time and we're concerned about the numbers you couldn't remember during the tests today. It might be crucial for a message like that to be remembered."

"I'm sorry," Noah said. "I'll try harder."

He felt his stomach lurch. He hadn't been thrilled with the idea of working for the government at first, but now he was determined to do it right.

"Too bad you didn't tell me the numbers," said Lena. "I still remember the list Dr. Odor asked me to repeat several weeks ago."

"Interesting that you would say that, Lena." Captain Billings came around his desk and sat on the edge. "We're going to spend your last day of training in a different way."

Noah blew out the air he had been holding in his lungs. It didn't sound like he was going to be fired.

"We've come up with several ways Noah can share thought information with you as a backup. Especially numbers." He looked directly at Noah. "You seem to do fine with words. It was the numbers that tripped you up."

Noah hated that he needed Lena to help him do his job. He turned to check her reaction.

"Sounds like a plan," said Lena. "When do we get started?"

"Right now," said Captain Billings. He walked behind the desk and pressed a button on his phone. The door opened and the same tech who had worked with Noah motioned for them to follow.

"I don't need your help!" Noah hissed at Lena.

"Looks like you do, Upchuck. Don't worry, I'll make you look good."

* * * * * *

The rest of the day, Noah practiced whispering messages to Lena after hearing the thoughts of the tech. They also worked on sign language. It frustrated Noah that Lena learned it faster than he had with a year of classes.

Captain Billings called them into the office for one last meeting before they went home.

"Congratulations to both of you on your hard work," he said. "When you get home, it will be essential to convince your parents you had a great time at Camp Wahuhi."

The captain slurped several gulps from his coffee cup. "You'll receive more information about the mission when we meet for a briefing before the trip to New York." Another gulp. He stood and paced the room. "During the next few weeks, both of you need to practice your Spanish and your sign language."

"No problem," Lena said.

Noah turned away when she grinned at him.

"Noah, we want you to continue practicing with the NT, but use caution. If we get word of you using it in a way that would be harmful to you or someone else…" He stopped pacing and stared at Noah. "Well, just don't do it."

He motioned for them to follow him to the waiting room.

It frustrated Noah that he couldn't use the NT when they were talking to the captain. He was sure details were being kept from him and Lena. Scary details.

"Until then," the captain said, "start school. Be normal."

Normal? Noah almost laughed out loud. He remembered wishing for normal before his cochlear had been activated. Normal would be worrying about the new school year, and teachers, and bullies in the hall.

How was he supposed to be normal after all this?

Chapter 26

"**S**o, Noah," Dad said, "tell us all about your camp." He wiped chicken grease from his fingers.

"Wait until I get dessert," Mom said. "I don't want to miss anything."

Tod groaned and started to leave.

Mom set a plate of cookies in the middle of the table, then pressed her hand on his shoulder to guide him back to his seat.

Noah made his last bite of Colonel's Chicken last as long as he could. Scanned his brain for something to say without giving away government secrets.

"I made a friend everyone called Einstein. He's beyond smart."

True statement.

"That's good," Mom said. "It seemed like there was a pretty little girl in a lot of your pictures too." She smiled. "Special friend?"

Little girl! If they saw Lena in action they wouldn't describe her as a little girl. More like a scary girl. Still Noah was glad Einstein sent several pictures of Lena and him together. Thought he might keep them on his phone.

"Not special," Noah said. "Just a friend." He searched for some way to change the direction of their questions. "The cookout was fun," he said and stuffed half a cookie in his mouth.

"Yes," Dad said, "we saw you really got into the marshmallows."

Noah's lips stretched into a grin when he remembered how he grossed out Lena with his mouth full for the picture.

"It's a wonder you didn't choke!" Mom said then took a sip of coffee.

Dad's laugh boomed across the table. "The trick is to breathe through your nose. Right, son?"

"Really? Next you'll be challenging one another to a contest," Mom said.

"Great idea!" Noah said.

"No. We're not having a food eating contest." Mom removed plates from the table.

"I have a question," said Tod.

"Sure, Tod," Dad said. "What's your question."

"How long do I have to sit here listening to little brother's glorious camp experience?" He slumped into his chair.

Dad folded his arms. He and Tod did a stare-down.

"Okay," Dad said after a few seconds, "you don't have to stay."

Noah reached behind his ear and clicked on the NT.

It's not like there's anything special going on in my life. Tod's sarcastic thoughts shouted into Noah's head.

"Hey, Tod," Noah said.

"What?" Tod leaned on the table.

"Anything new at football practice while I was gone?"

A little flick of Tod's eyebrows said as much as his thoughts. *You mean the not important news that Coach put me on the starting team?*

"Oh, that's right," said Dad. "Your coach was going to post the starting list today? Did you make it?"

Tod gave a half smile and said, "Yeah. No big deal though."

"Of course it's a big deal." Dad stood and put his hand out for a high-five. "Really proud of you, son."

Noah gave him a thumbs up. For once he was grateful for the mix-up with the cochlear. Glad he was able to hear past the jerk attitude his brother showed most of the time. He smiled and pictured a time when they could be close again.

"What are you laughing about, jerk?" Tod asked, then shoved past him.

Close? Ha! Not yet.

* * * * * *

After days convincing his parents how cool Camp Wahuhi was, Noah was relieved when school started. The parent fifth degree changed to, "How are your classes?" and "Make any new friends?"

He did make a few friends since he could sort of keep up with their conversations at lunch. Most kids gave him weird looks and pointed at his cochlear, but eventually they ignored him. Just like before.

It was tempting to listen to thoughts at school, but he forced himself to practice only at home and a few times at the mall. After what the captain said, Noah wondered if the government had inserted some kind of device in his cochlear to keep track of how he used it. Noah shivered at the thought of having someone inside his head.

Kind of how people would feel if they knew he was inside theirs.

Chapter 27

...0800 hours...

New York City Pre-Mission Training.

"Buenos dias, señor Noah," Lena said as Noah crawled into the backseat beside her.

Noah thought it was kinda great to see her. They'd spent most of their time at camp arguing, but still, she sorta felt like a friend. She even smiled.

Smiles can be deceiving.

"¿Cualquier plan para vomitar hoy?" *Any plan to throw up today?*

"Very funny," Noah said.

He wasn't sure what she said, but he recognized a word that sounded like vomit. "Te lo haré saber." *I will let you know.*

Lena's eyes widened. "I'm impressed, Upchuck."

And then she blew a bubble and popped it two inches from his face.

"Okay, kids," Lieutenant Green said as he turned with his palm out. "Cell phones please."

Lena groaned. "You don't know how horrible this is for me."

The lieutenant didn't seem concerned. He snapped his fingers and flattened his palm like he did before. Two cell phones were handed to him. "Why don't you practice sign language while we drive to our meeting. You know, without talking out loud."

"Do you know sign language, Lieutenant Green?" Lena asked.

"No, Lena, I don't," he answered.

"Good!"

Noah laughed.

Lieutenant Green gave them an annoyed look and raised the thick glass between the front and back seats.

"Good one, Lena!" Noah said and signed the words at the same time.

Lena's eyes opened wide. "Hey, that's pretty good. You've been practicing."

"Well," Noah said and shrugged his shoulders. "I'm not without skills."

He should have been better than her since he'd been practicing for the last year. But he knew, being better than Lena was almost impossible.

Lena turned to the window and Noah heard the robotic sound of several bubbles pinging off the glass.

He tapped her on the shoulder and signed, "Were your parents convinced about Camp Wahuhi?"

"I think so," she signed. "How about you?"

Noah nodded, then said out loud, "It was sad how excited they were. Made me feel bad for not telling them the whole thing was fake."

Lena nodded and turned away from him.

"Lena, I've been thinking about how Captain Billings wants me to tell you numbers when I read someone's thoughts."

"And...?" she asked in her normal sarcastic tone.

"I understand whispering numbers and stuff to you, but what if we aren't close enough to do that?" Noah rubbed his palms on his pants. "It just seems kind of strange that they would want us to sign. Other people know sign language too."

"I wondered about that." More bubbles popped. "Maybe we should…"

Lena hesitated and pointed to the speakers in the ceiling. She signed the next words: *come up with our own signals. Maybe a code.*

Noah gave her an exaggerated nod.

"I'll work on it," she said out loud.

Noah watched as Lena scribbled on a blank page in the back of her notebook. He wanted to ask her a question but hated to interrupt her. She was in the zone.

"Lena, we're almost at the hospital," he finally said.

She held up her index finger. Just as the car pulled onto the circle drive, Lena ripped the page from her notebook.

"No time to talk. Memorize this." She handed him the paper and shoved the notebook into her backpack.

Noah did a quick scan of numbers, words, and hand sign pictures on the page. As much as he hated to admit it, Lena was brilliant. Now, if he could get all this in his head.

"And Noah…" Lena whispered, then hesitated.

"What?" he asked with a glance away from the page. Lena's worried expression made his stomach lurch.

She whispered, "They've got secrets. So do we."

* * * * * *

"Okay, Noah and Lena," said Einstein, the tech guy from Camp Alpha, "these phones are for you to use in New York. The captain wants you to send pictures to your parents like you normally would on a school trip. He said to act like normal kids."

There was that normal thing again.

"Why can't I use my own phone?" Lena asked.

Einstein made a quirky smirk and said, "Because these are secure phones and your personal phone is not."

He picked up his laptop and started for the door. "You two stay here. One of the techs will be continuing your training in a few."

The same tech from the camp walked into the training room with her signature clipboard. "Good morning, Noah and Lena. Do you need a break or are you ready to get started?"

Noah glanced at Lena. She said, "We're okay. Ready to get this over with."

The tech twisted her mouth like she wasn't pleased with Lena's attitude. "Very well, Noah, listen to my thoughts and then sign the information to Lena."

She switched on a video camera in the corner to record their training.

Noah was tempted to use some of Lena's signs just to see if the tech was paying attention. Decided he better not.

They spent several hours practicing the same drill over and over. Sometimes the thoughts were in English. Sometimes Spanish. Sometimes a mix. The tech's English thoughts always had an odd accent. Just like they did at camp. It bugged him, but he let it go.

The tech added to her notes and said, "Again. Listen to my thoughts and sign to Lena what you hear."

Noah nodded and waited for the brain tingle. His forehead wrinkled in concentration.

"I'm waiting, Upchuck."

Noah could tell Lena was itching for a piece of gum and it was making her grumpy.

He closed his eyes and did a head translation of the Spanish words and numbers into English. He turned to Lena and his fingers started moving.

"Got it!" Lena said. "I hope he did."

"What did he say?" asked the tech.

"Location is 7.63222 by 66.1611."

The tech typed notes on her laptop. Noah scrubbed his palms on his thighs while Lena twisted her braid.

"Did she get it right?" Noah asked.

"Of course, I got it right! The question is, did you?"

The tech shut the laptop and punched numbers into her cell phone.

"We're finished," she said into the phone. "Yes, sir." She slipped the phone in her lab coat pocket and stood.

"Aren't you going to tell us how we did?" Noah asked.

"Not my job. Dr. Odor and Captain Billings will give you the final report. Follow me."

Noah smelled the grape gum before they had walked five steps. "You better chew quick. Remember what Lieutenant Green said about gum."

"You take care of those sweaty hands," Lena mumbled through her wad of gum, "and I'll take care of my gum."

Noah felt his face glow. He fell a few steps behind and scrubbed his hands on his jeans.

Lieutenant Green was waiting with a grin and a trashcan outside the office. "I'll take it from here. Everybody ready?"

He opened the door.

Noah wondered if the training had worked or would there be a Plan C?

"Oh, good," said Dr. Odor when they entered the room. "Here's our team, now."

The smell of the doctor's cologne hadn't improved. Noah couldn't resist covering his nose. He wondered how it wasn't bothering everyone else.

Captain Billings motioned for them to sit in the two chairs facing the desk where he sat. His caterpillar eyebrows jumped above his dark rimmed glasses like they had before. Dr. Odor and Lieutenant Green stood to the side.

"Let's proceed, Doctor," said the captain. "This team has a flight to catch."

Noah thought that was a good sign. The mission was still going to happen. At least he thought that was good.

Dr. Odor cleared his throat. "Of course."

He revealed his uneasiness as he shuffled papers and clicked his pen several times. "Noah and Lena have passed the tests with flying colors!"

Noah let out the breath he had trapped in his lungs. He was surprised when Lena held up her open hand. He slapped it with his own. He couldn't hold in a laugh when she used several of their private signs to make fun of Dr. Odor's awful cologne.

The captain cleared his throat and stood. "As I said before." He planted his fists on the desk and glared at them. "I do hope you are both taking this seriously."

"I'm sure they are, Captain." Dr. Odor walked behind Noah and squeezed his shoulders. "These kids have worked very hard. They won't let you down."

Noah winced as the doctor's fingers squeezed harder.

Lena moved to sit on the edge of her seat. "Sorry, sir. We know this is important. I'll make sure Noah doesn't mess up."

Noah glared at her and started to argue, but her thoughts came screaming at him. He swallowed hard when he realized he'd forgotten to shut off the NT.

Just chill! I'm trying to get us out of here.

Noah relaxed and gave her a slight thumbs up.

"That's very reassuring, Lena." The captain stood and walked around the desk. "We're counting on both of you to watch out for each other."

He reached his hand out to shake their hands. "Your gear has already been loaded. Lieutenant Green and Corporal Powell are waiting at the car. Good luck."

"Just one moment," said Dr. Odor. "I'd like to make a quick check of Noah's cochlear processor before the mission. Shouldn't take five minutes."

"Certainly," said Captain Billings. "Lena you can sit in the waiting room. Just bring Noah back here when you're finished."

Noah could feel sweat almost drip off his hands. He glanced at Lena. The last time there was one more check of his processor was when Dr. Odor almost threatened him.

What would be the threat this time?

Chapter 28

"You can have a seat on the exam table, Noah," Dr. Odor said. He pulled on gloves and removed Noah's cochlear processor.

"Why are you checking it?" Noah asked. "The tech spent forever with it hooked up to a computer this morning."

The doctor's lips were moving while he turned the processor over and over in his hand. Noah felt his heart speed up in his chest when the doctor hesitated near the NT button.

"…you…ready…for…," the doctor's lips said.

Noah raised his palms and his shoulders. "I don't understand."

Dr. Odor said, "Sorry."

He held up his index finger.

Noah felt the click of the processor being reattached and the microphone earpiece fitting behind his ear. Sound was immediate— the whosh of the air conditioner, the rattling of paper on the exam table, the doctor clearing his throat. It still amazed Noah that the electronic sounds were becoming recognizable to him. More every day.

"How's that?" the doctor asked.

Noah held up his thumb and waited for what he was sure was next.

"Good!" said Dr. Odor. "What I said was, I want to make sure your cochlear is ready for the mission."

The doctor produced a toothy grin.

Definitely forced.

"I think I'm good. We've been practicing. We're ready," Noah nodded and waited.

"Good to know. But, Noah, I noticed you and Lena using sign language."

"Sure," Noah said. "That's part of the plan."

"Well," Dr. Odor hesitated and clicked his pen, "I didn't recognize some of the signs."

Noah's felt his face heat. He waited for the brain tingle of the doctor's thoughts.

Nothing.

The NT had been shut off.

He squirmed making the exam table crackle under him. He wondered what Dr. Odor didn't want him to hear. Lena's instructions about their secret code haunted him. *Don't tell anyone, Noah.*

"Sorry, Dr. Odor, I'm not as good as I should be at the signs." He pressed his lips together and tried to look humiliated.

"Sure," the doctor said as he stared out the window, "I realize that. But it was Lena who made some signs that weren't recognizable."

He leaned in close and stared. "Lena rarely makes mistakes. Are you and Lena making a joke out of this mission? We've guaranteed Captain Billings that you are not."

Noah stared at a picture of the American flag on the wall. He focused his eyes back on Dr. Odor's frowning face.

"No jokes. We're ready," he said almost in a whisper.

"Just remember, Noah, there are some great rewards for you and your family." The doctor stood and walked to the door. "There are also risks. Risks for all of us."

He opened the door and motioned for him to leave.

Noah hopped from the table and tried to keep his legs from trembling. "I know. You told me that before." He walked through the door, then turned back. "We'll do what we're supposed to do. I promise."

It took all of Noah's control to walk away and not run. He needed to talk to Lena, but he was getting more and more paranoid about hidden cameras and recording devices. It was creepy. While he navigated the halls to where Lena waited, he scratched his head near the cochlear and activated the NT.

As expected, Lena was doing her bubble thing in the waiting room. Her eyes opened wide when she saw him. Noah tapped his temple—their signal for Lena to send him thoughts.

You look scared, Upchuck. What happened? She thought.

Noah leaned in and whispered, "We need to talk without ears and eyes."

"Let's go," she said.

Noah followed Lena.

"Where are you going?" he asked.

Her thoughts jumped into Noah's mind. *The bathroom. Remember?*

Noah saw the LADIES room sign and said, "No way!"

Again, she sent her thoughts. *This is the closest one. Next time we'll go in the men's room.*

Noah wanted to argue. Knew there wasn't time. He locked the door after they entered. Lena immediately turned on the faucet.

"Spill it, Upchuck."

"Dr. Odor noticed our made-up sign language."

"What did you say to him?" Lena asked.

"I told him it was because I wasn't very good at it. He said he knew that, but that you didn't make mistakes."

Lena smiled as she popped her gum and mumbled around it. "Well, that's true."

"He thinks we're making a joke out of the mission. At least, I think that's what he meant." Noah put his hands on top of his head. "What are we going to do?"

"We just need to be careful. Just use the symbols I gave you and not the made-up signs." The sound of her popping gum bounced off the bathroom walls. "Unless you think we can trust Dr. Odor."

"I wish we could, but he keeps making those threats about the risks everyone is taking."

"Okay, let's go before they start looking for us."

She unlocked the door and peeked into the hall. "All clear. Go."

They barely made it into the hall when Lieutenant Green's voiced boomed from an open door. "Where have you two been? We're already behind schedule."

"Sorry, Lieutenant," Lena said. "Noah got lost on his way back from Dr. Odor checking his cochlear."

"What?" Noah started to say when he got a brain tingle.

Sorry, Noah. Just go with it. Lena thought.

"I get it," said the lieutenant. "But let's hustle. Captain Billings is going to have my hide if you two don't make that flight."

Chapter 29

"How come you get the window seat?" Lena asked.

Noah held his boarding pass close to her face. "My name, my seat."

It felt good to be one up on her for once. He caved when he saw the disappointment in her eyes. "Don't worry. We can trade back and forth."

Outside the window, workers were loading luggage and pulling hoses from the plane. Noah's stomach did a roller coaster roll at the thought of his first flight. Before the accident he'd been ecstatic when his family was making plans to fly to California. Before and after.

The trip was canceled.

He never asked why, but he knew.

"I'll trade after take-off. I want to see if I can spot my house."

"You won't," Lena said as she popped a piece of gum in her mouth.

"How do you know?" Noah regretted his question as soon as Lena started a lecture about the direction they would be banking and why.

Lieutenant Green stood and dug through his carry-on bag, then dropped into the aisle seat beside Lena. It was weird to see him in jeans and a cool shirt instead of his uniform.

"Here!" He slapped packets in each of their laps. "There won't be much gazing out the window, Noah. Captain Billings sent you important information to review before we land."

"Really?" Noah asked. "My head is about to explode with all the stuff now."

The lieutenant leaned toward them and spoke in low tones, "Don't forget. You have jobs to do."

He stared at Noah for an uncomfortable amount of time. "Don't discuss the information in your packets out loud. That can wait until we are in the hotel where the rooms have been swept for listening devices."

Our listening devices or someone else's? Noah heard Lena think.

"Yeah, right," Noah said out loud.

"Right, what?" Lieutenant Green asked.

"Oh, nothing," Noah said. "Just listening."

He glanced at Lena and she gave him a rare smile.

"Shut it off, Noah. You don't need the distraction." The lieutenant tapped the manila envelope in Noah's hands. "Give this information your full attention. If you need to discuss something, use your sign language. You know, silently! Oh, and Lena, first bubble I hear and your gum is gone. Noah, I believe Dr. Odor included instructions about your device in the packet. Read and heed."

He laughed, but stopped when he realized the lieutenant wasn't trying to be funny.

Lieutenant Green sat back and mumbled something to Corporal Powell across the aisle. Noah couldn't understand it, but he caught the meaning. What was making him so grumpy?

The hour and a half flight to JFK Airport *could* have been exciting, amazing.

But it reminded Noah too much of school. Lieutenant Green even pulled down the window shade so they could "concentrate."

In the packets, they found a picture of Marcos Barbosa, the Viracochan Ambassador to the United Nations. Noah nudged Lena. He tapped the picture and then his temple. She nodded, understanding that this was the man. There were also pictures of several advisers to the ambassador. Noah felt overwhelmed by the bios on all the people. He rested his head in his hands and groaned. Why did he agree to do this?

"What's wrong?" Lena asked. "You're not going to hurl are you?"

She grabbed the airsick back from the seat pocket.

Noah looked up and reached for her arm. "No, I'm not sick."

He signed the rest to her. *What if they don't think in English? My Spanish isn't great. I don't want to mess up.*

"You won't, Noah."

Wow, a real moment. Lena never called him anything but Upchuck.

Lena flipped her hair. "But if you do, I'll be there to fix it."

Bonding moment gone. "How are you going to fix it?"

Lena signed, *If they think in Spanish, just remember what you can and I'll interpret. Easy.*

It sounded easy when she said it, but Noah wasn't so sure. He unbuckled his seat belt and said, "Let me out. Restroom."

Lena pulled her legs back and tapped the lieutenant on the shoulder. "Noah's gotta go."

The lieutenant moved from his seat to the aisle. "Make it quick, Noah. Landing soon."

Noah nodded. He navigated the narrow aisle toward the front of the plane and through the first class section. The OCCUPIED sign was showing on the restroom door so he leaned against the metal galley wall and waited. The flight attendant smiled and kept working. The smell of first class hot cookies made his mouth water.

A man seated on the aisle looked up at the attendant then stared in Noah's direction. He looked familiar. Dark hair. Little mustache.

Noah searched his memory. Since he was in first class, maybe he was a movie star or something. The man's newspaper snapped in front of his face as soon as he noticed Noah was watching.

It took a while for Noah to figure out how to flush the toilet. The blue water kinda freaked him out. He glanced in the mirror while he was washing his hands. It was still a shock when he saw the cochlear fastened to the side of his head. He turned his head and imagined devices on both sides. Just before he slid the lock on the door, he decided to turn on the NT. It was worth going against the lieutenant's orders to check out the staring man.

He slipped out the small door and past the lady who was waiting in line. He forced himself not to look directly at the mustache man as he came near his seat. From the side of his vision he could tell the man was still watching. Noah searched through the wave of thoughts that rushed at him. He finally turned to stare directly at the man. His thought words floated to the top.

He doesn't look that special to me. Must be the girl.

If Noah had gum in his mouth he was sure he would have swallowed it. Even a stranger thinks Lena is better than him. But how did he know about them at all. The man's thoughts were in English but he had the same accent he heard in the tech's thoughts during training. Noah tripped his way back to his seat and debated whether to tell Lieutenant Green or not. The lieutenant would get mad if he knew Noah hadn't followed orders. Lena was his best bet. He couldn't keep this to himself.

Lieutenant Green put his earphones in his carry-on in the overhead compartment while Noah moved to his seat. Before the lieutenant noticed, Noah signed to Lena, "Aisle 6-C."

She looked confused for a second then excused herself to go to the restroom.

"Not sure you have time, Lena," said the lieutenant.

"Can't wait." She sprinted to the front of the plane.

One of the flight attendants leaned toward the lieutenant. "Sir, please ask your daughter not to run in the aisle."

"Oh, sure. Sorry." Lieutenant Green glanced at Corporal Powell across the aisle.

He turned to Noah. "Didn't you kids receive instruction about how NOT to draw attention to yourselves?"

"Hey!" Noah replied. "She's the one who ran, not me."

For once, Lena goofed up, but he still got a chewing. Noah scrubbed his palms on his pants while he waited for her to return.

"Ladies and gentlemen, we will be landing at JFK in the next ten minutes. Please return to your seats, return tray tables to their upright and locked position, and buckle your seat belts. One of the attendants will be making one more pass for any trash you might have. Thank you for flying with us."

Lena was back before Noah could get the sweat rubbed off his palms.

She slipped into her seat and tapped her temple. *Weird guy. Kept staring at me.*

Noah signed, *Did he look familiar?*

No, Lena thought. *Have you seen him before?*

Yes. Noah signed.

The plane began dropping lower in the sky. Noah flipped up the shade. The skyline of New York filled the window. He didn't know if it was excitement that made his heart race or worrying about the man in first class.

Not that special. Must be the girl.

Chapter 30

The plane landed and Noah and Lena were rushed to a waiting car. The tech from training was waiting in the back for one more practice session.

Noah's curiosity won out and he asked the tech, "What's the other language you speak?"

"What makes you think I speak another language?" she asked.

"Your thoughts. They have an accent. What language is it?"

"Fascinating. Hmmm…My parents were missionaries in Brazil. I grew up speaking Portuguese." She stared at Noah with a confused expression, then scribbled something in her notes. "Dr. Odor is going to find this fascinating."

The car jerked to a stop and the side door opened. The noise level from the streets of the city made Noah pull back.

"What's wrong, Upchuck?" asked Lena as she crawled over him to use the sidewalk side of the car.

Noah followed her. "It's so loud!"

He struggled to sort his own words from the chaos.

"Get used to it," Lieutenant Green said then guided them into the hotel. "This city never sleeps."

They entered the lobby through a revolving door. "Leave your gear with Corporal Powell. She'll get it to our rooms."

Noah turned in circles. Tried to take in the whole lobby. Glass, steel, huge vases of flowers, polished floors and walls made of what he thought was marble. He felt a hand on his back, guiding him to the elevator.

"No time to be a tourist, Noah. We have a briefing in Captain Billings's suite in five minutes."

Lieutenant Green barely pushed number 27 before he turned to them and said, "I know this is a lot to take in. I can't encourage you enough to NOT draw extra attention to yourselves. Blend in as much as possible." He gave a half smile. "I know it doesn't seem like it, but I think you're kinda great kids. Wouldn't want you hurt."

No one spoke as the elevator went higher and higher. As much as Noah wanted this to be a fun adventure, he was constantly reminded of the dangers. The doors opened and an electronic voice said, "Twenty-seventh floor."

Lieutenant Green held a tissue for Lena's gum then motioned for them both to go first. Two military guards stood on either side of the elevator. Double doors opened on a room directly across from the elevator. Noah's nose wrinkled from the doctor's strong cologne before he heard his voice.

"Greetings Team," said Dr. Odor. A forced smile stretched across his face. "Welcome to your first mission."

"Wow!" Noah and Lena said at the same time.

The room was huge with windows on two sides. Buildings towered in the streets outside. Some looked familiar. Noah thought he should have known their names. Wished he could look them up on his phone. Several people were working at computers. Wires crisscrossed the floor and computers sat on every surface—even the bar. Einstein gave them a two-finger salute. Noah smiled.

"Come this way, Team."

"Dr. Odor's acting weird, like he's the host or something," whispered Lena.

Noah nodded. "The captain makes him nervous."

"Captain Billings," Dr. Odor continued, "Noah and Lena have arrived."

The doctor stood waiting for a response from the captain, who sat frowning.

At the only desk in the room.

Ignoring the doctor.

"Lieutenant Green," barked the captain.

"Yes, sir." The lieutenant stepped forward and saluted.

The captain returned the salute. "At ease, Lieutenant."

The captain motioned for them to all sit in the chairs in front of his desk. There wasn't a seat for the doctor. He backed away and sat on a couch across the room.

"Congratulations, Lieutenant, for getting the team here safely. Any problems?"

"No, sir." Lieutenant Green glanced at Noah and Lena. "No incidents."

Noah felt a brain tingle. He'd forgotten to turn off the NT. Lena's thoughts broke through his own.

Tell about the man. Lena stared at him with her eyebrows raised.

Noah shook his head, then scrubbed his palms.

"Is there something you want to add, Noah?" the captain's voice boomed.

Noah squirmed in his seat. Wondered if he'd be in trouble for activating the NT on the plane. Remembered the order to never leave it activated in a meeting with the captain. It seemed like he was always breaking someone's instructions.

Lena scooted to the edge of her seat. "Yes, Captain. Noah saw something on the plane."

"Thanks a lot," Noah muttered.

"Somebody has to give you a push," Lena responded.

"Lieutenant Green, can you enlighten us on this?"

147

Noah regretted not telling the lieutenant about the man sooner. Didn't feel good about getting him in trouble.

"No, sir," said the lieutenant. "This is the first I'm hearing about it. Spit it out. Remember our conversation on the track? No secrets."

Noah wanted to laugh. Like they weren't keeping things from Lena and him. He took a deep breath. "Well, there was this man on the plane who kept staring at me."

"Where was he seated?" the lieutenant asked.

"First Class, 6-C. I saw him while I was waiting for the restroom. He tried to cover his face with a newspaper." Part of Noah felt relief he was telling it. Another part dreaded what was coming. "Lena saw him, too."

"One of ours?" Captain Billings asked an aide standing beside him.

"No, sir. Our people were scattered throughout the plane, but the one in front was a female."

Noah's thoughts agreed with Lena's. *How come we didn't know about the other people?*

He looked at her and nodded. Dumb mistake.

Lieutenant Green noticed. "Shut off the NT, Noah."

There was an edge to his voice.

Noah pushed the button. "There's something else. It may not be important."

More palm swipes on his thighs.

"We need to know it all. The smallest detail could affect the mission," said the captain.

"Lieutenant Green said to leave the NT off while we were on the plane. He said I didn't need the distraction." Noah glanced at the lieutenant and squirmed. "But, when I saw the man staring, I wanted to know what he was thinking."

"And what were his thoughts?" Captain Billings asked.

"He thought I didn't seem that special and that it must be the girl." Noah blew out his breath. "And he had an accent."

"An accent? You talked to him?" asked the captain.

"No. His thoughts had an accent." Noah tried to swallow the tension in his throat. "Just like the tech did at our training. The one that rode with us in the car to the hotel."

Dr. Odor cleared his throat from the couch and stood. "That would be Technician Wilson." He walked toward the captain's desk. "We have discovered that Noah can distinguish accents in thoughts. We feel this will be an added benefit to his abilities."

Lena glanced at Noah. He didn't need the NT to be active to know she was thinking the same as him. Dr. Odor was trying to take credit for something Noah had just told the tech in the car.

"We need a copy of the manifest passenger list from the airlines," said Captain Billings.

Einstein stepped forward. "Done."

He set a paper on the captain's desk.

"In the meantime," the captain said as he scanned the paper, "do they have clean cell phones?"

"They do, Captain Billings," said the lieutenant.

"Good. Give them some pointers on getting a picture without looking too obvious."

"Yes, sir," said Lieutenant Green.

The captain faced Noah and Lena. "We'll be monitoring you at all times, but since you are the only two who know what he looks like, it might be necessary for you to get a picture if he shows up again." The captain looked over the top of his glasses. "Both of you, pay attention to what Lieutenant Green told you. You see something, you tell us."

The urgency in the captain's voice pushed Noah toward panic. "Yes, sir."

"Now, get a good night's sleep." He focused again on the passenger list, then stared at them over his glasses.

"Everybody stay sharp. Things just got complicated."

Chapter 31

N oah studied the purple lanyard he was handed at the registration table when he and Lena entered the hotel meeting room the next morning. "Did it have to be purple?"

Lena blew a bubble and held her lanyard beside it. She popped the bubble and asked, "Does it match?"

"Way too much," Noah said as they found their place cards at one of the round tables.

He sat and took a sip of the orange juice beside his plate. A combination of kids, chaperones, and adults in suits sat or stood around the room. Noah wondered if there were any government protectors in there besides Lieutenant Green and Corporal Powell.

Wished he could have turned his NT on to find out.

Lena was talking to the girl beside her who had an artificial arm. The kid next to Noah wore sunglasses. His hand rested on a guide dog by his chair. Noah tried to think what to say to him when the boy spoke.

"You're not supposed to pet him, but he's not working now, so it's okay with me." The boy reached his hand toward Noah. "Hi, my name's Miguel. Bet you can't guess what my disability is."

Noah laughed and shook the boy's hand. "Hi! I'm Noah."

"May I have your attention, please?" A very official looking lady welcomed everyone and started her long a speech about how brave they all were to face their disabilities with courage.

Lena tapped Noah on the arm and made a gagging motion with her finger in her mouth.

Lieutenant Green shot them a stern look from his nearby table.

Noah wished the lieutenant would let his sense of humor return. On the other hand, he did like the idea of having someone around who had his back.

After breakfast, they loaded into a couple buses for a fast tour of the city. Noah and Lena stayed together like they were told. It almost felt like a real school trip with new friends. Normal even. But that feeling changed when Noah saw someone who jerked him back to the mission.

They had finished the Empire State Building tour and were unloading for a tour of the 9/11 Memorial. Noah stepped off the bus behind Miguel and his dog. He pretended he didn't notice the man from the plane, but he was there. Sitting on a park bench with his trusty newspaper.

"Lena, don't look, but a friend of ours is at nine o'clock on the bench."

She nodded and said in a high pitched girly voice. "Hey, Noah, let's get a selfie!"

Miguel spoke up, "I'd offer to take it for you, but, well…you know."

He pointed at his eyes.

Lena smiled and grabbed Noah to stand beside her. "That's okay, Miguel. We've got it." She held the camera way higher than she should have, but she got a clear shot of the man when he dropped the newspaper from his face.

"Got it!" She punched a few buttons and immediately sent it to the number Lieutenant Green gave them. "Let's go."

They ran to catch the other kids. Noah glanced back, but the man was gone.

It didn't make him feel any less uneasy.

Lieutenant Green and Corporal Powell must have seen the picture and note Lena sent. They placed themselves behind Noah and Lena as they viewed the two waterfall pools and almost three thousand names of lives lost on 9/11/01.

"Hey, Lena," Noah whispered as they waited to load the bus after the tour. "Remember when we talked about why we're doing this thing?"

"Uh-huh. Why?" Lena asked.

Noah pointed to the space where the Twin Towers used to stand watch above the city. "That's why I'm doing this."

Lena nodded and said in a tight voice, "Yeah, me too."

Noah looked away to hide the tears that stung his eyes. He was sorry his dad wasn't there—hoped they could someday see it together.

The bus brought the group back to the hotel. They were herded into the same room where they had breakfast. The face of the man with the newspaper flitted in and out of Noah's thoughts while he pretended he was listening to instructions about United Nations protocol for the next day. It was information he and Lena had already learned in their training. Instead, he scanned his memory of where he had seen the little mustache and the piercing eyes before.

After they were dismissed for the day, Noah followed Lena from the room. He felt a tap on his shoulder.

"Some of us are going to check out the hotel pool. Wanna go?" Miguel asked. "You too, Lena."

Noah wished he had the courage to ignore Lieutenant Green's stern head shake. More meetings with Captain Billings or training were probably the only entertainment they were going to have.

"Sounds great! But…"

He couldn't say they had meetings about their secret mission and the creepy guy that was following them. Noah searched for an excuse that sounded believable.

Lena leaned around him and said, "That would be fun, Miguel. But one of our sponsors wants to take us to some fancy restaurant. I know. Sounds boring."

Miguel looked disappointed. "Okay, maybe tomorrow after we go to the UN."

"You got it," said Noah.

Lieutenant Green guided them toward the elevator. After the doors closed, he said, "Good cover, Lena." He pressed the button for the twenty-seventh floor. "Now, let's go meet with your *sponsor* before I get busted to a private."

* * * * * *

They spent the rest of the evening practicing with a tech and reviewing information about the Viracochan Ambassador, Marcos Barbosa. Noah asked several times, but no one would tell him anything about the man that was following them.

"We've got it all under control, Noah," said Captain Billings. "You just concentrate on the mission."

That answer didn't make Noah feel any less nervous when they were finally allowed to go to their rooms. He knew it was important to sleep, but he couldn't shut off his mind. The thoughts he heard from the man with the piercing eyes looped over and over.

Doesn't look that special to me. Must be the girl.

Must be the girl.

Must be the girl.

Chapter 32

"How does that feel?" Einstein said as he fitted Noah and Lena with hidden wires and microphones early the next morning.

"Weird," said Noah.

"We're good," said Lena as she straightened the collar of her polo shirt that matched his. "Noah, are you okay?"

"No," Noah muttered and wondered why Lena was being so nice. "I couldn't sleep last night. I just want this to be over."

"It's going to be fine. You do your listening thing, I'll make you look good by remembering what you hear, then we'll go home. Easy-peasey."

Ahhh, Noah thought. That's the Lena I know.

"Everybody ready?" Lieutenant Green poked his head around the edge of the door.

"You bet!" Lena said.

"I guess," Noah mumbled.

The lieutenant patted him on the back. "You've got this, kid. Just get as close to the ambassador as you can and do your thing."

Noah nodded and followed to the elevator.

* * * * *

A cool wind blew across the East River mixing a fishy smell with exhaust from the constant traffic beside the United Nations Building. Noah noticed Lena had an odd expression on her face as they filed off the bus on East 42nd Street with the rest of their group. She kept looking toward the river and held her hand in front of her nose and mouth.

"You okay?" he asked.

"Of course," she said and glanced toward the United Nations building. "There it is."

"Yep," Noah responded. "It looks like a giant cell phone stuck in the ground."

"Hey, you're right," said Lena. "Amazing flags though."

While all the kids were positioned for a group photo, Noah scanned the hundreds of tourists and workers moving around the fountains and statues in front of the building. No sign of the man he saw on the plane and on the bench the day before.

"Hey, Noah," Miguel said behind him. "Dare you to make a funny face in the next picture."

It was tempting but Noah saw Lieutenant Green's serious scowl nearby. He remembered the instructions not to draw attention.

"Don't do it, Noah," Lena hissed.

"I'm not an idiot," Noah said through a smile that would make his mom proud.

They were handed visitor badges, then given a brief tour of the lobby. After the tour, the guide read visitor conduct rules while in the General Assembly.

Noah elbowed Lena and said, "Guess you noticed they said no gum."

Lena responded with a typical eye roll then pushed him into the line to enter the massive room. Row after row of long curved tables and seats faced a platform where a woman was reading a speech in a language Noah didn't recognize. He was surprised how muffled sound was through his cochlear. The people sitting at the tables all had earphones covering their ears but according to their moving lips, many were talking to those beside them. Again, he wished his dad was with him. Knew he would think this was the coolest thing ever.

After the speaker finished and polite applause pattered across the room, the disabled children were introduced and asked to stand. Noah felt his face heat as hundreds of heads turned toward them and acknowledged their presence with more hand clapping.

"This is weird," he whispered to Lena.

"What do you mean?" She waved and nodded to the smiling faces. "I think it's cool!"

An escort led the group from the room and they were divided into smaller meetings with individual ambassadors. Lieutenant Green and Corporal Powell guided Noah and Lena into a wood paneled room where Noah immediately recognized the Viracochan Ambassador, Marcos Barbosa.

"Ambassador Barbosa," an American UN Aide said, "I'd like you to meet Lena Robinson and Noah Baker."

Noah stepped forward and shook the ambassador's hand.

Lena shook his hand and said, "Buenos dias, Ambassador Barbosa."

She turned and smirked at Noah.

He was glad he couldn't hear her snide thoughts. That's when he remembered his orders to turn on the NT after the General Assembly. Reaching to scratch his head, he clicked the button. A bombardment of thoughts took his breath. English and other languages mixed with robotic words that pinged off the tall ceiling of the meeting room. Noah felt overwhelmed and fought panic. He let Lena talk and concentrated on sorting the different voices.

Must stay on schedule.

Forgot I have that reception this evening.

Words with an accent like his training tech floated to the top. Noah noticed the ambassador hold his stomach and wince.

Meu estomago! American food does not agree.

Slowly Noah moved closer to Barbosa. He nodded to Lena to signal he was ready.

"Ambassador Barbosa," Lena said, "we'd like to discuss the importance of helping disabled children in your country."

"Ah, yes, a very worthy project," said Ambassador Barbosa. "We appreciate the assistance your government has sent to help our unfortunate children."

"Of course," said the American Aide.

Noah struggled to listen to the conversation and still concentrate on the ambassador's thoughts. He was amazed how insignificant the thoughts were. As if the man was completely bored with his job.

Then the American Aide changed the direction of the conversation. "We'd like to discuss another area of concern for our country as well as yours."

Everyone was directed to an area with chairs in a circle. Noah rubbed his fingers back and forth on the seam of the leather chair where he was seated. Ambassador Barbosa sat directly across from him. Noah tried to stay focused rather than give into his nerves.

The American Aide continued, "Noah and Lena are concerned with the injuries to children in your country due to the civil war that is occurring."

This is it. Noah waited.

"Of course, of course," said Barbosa. "As are we concerned. The damage and injuries caused by the bombings is disturbing to our government. Our best people are working on a solution to end the conflict."

Those were the words he said, but his thoughts said the complete opposite.

Asombroso! Such pompous people.

No longer concerned about his stomach, the ambassador's thoughts gained power. Almost as if he was shouting.

Viracocha does not need the United States telling us the war is a concern. We will settle the rebellion without your help.

The American Aide moved forward in his seat. "We have another concern of which we believe you are already aware."

"And what would that be?" Ambassador said with a sneer.

"We have received information that the rebels in your civil war have taken several U.S. citizens as prisoners. We believe they are hoping the United States will get involved in the war."

The Viracochan Ambassador stood. "I know nothing of the rebels' plans, and I assure you the government of Viracocha has no need for your involvement."

Noah searched the ambassador's thoughts to see if he was lying. His words were a jumble of Spanish and English, but it didn't seem to Noah that he was thinking anything different from what he was saying.

"Excuse me, Ambassador," one of the Viracochan aides Noah hadn't noticed moved forward. She leaned to whisper in the ambassador's ear. There was some nodding then she backed away.

That's when the woman's thoughts pushed aside the words of the ambassador and shouted in Noah's head.

Of course, you know nothing of our plans, but my rebel brothers and sisters will control the Viracochan government soon. She put her hands behind her back and narrowed her eyes. *You foolish old man!* She glanced at her watch. *A truck is moving the prisoners from San Rafael to the mountains in Merida within the hour. Then we will no doubt involve the United States.*

The accent was strong, but Noah was sure what he heard. He nodded to Lieutenant Green and repeated the words over and over in his head. When the conversation continued, Noah waited for a lull and pushed to the edge of his seat. He reached his hand to the man who made his skin crawl.

"Thank you, Ambassador Barbosa," Noah said. "Lena and I are very grateful you were willing to meet with us."

Everyone stood. The American Aide nodded to Lieutenant Green and said to Ambassador Barbosa, "I have a few other topics to discuss with you."

Lieutenant Green led the kids from the meeting.

Noah didn't think he would forget but he whispered San Rafael and Merida, to Lena, just in case.

The lobby was filled with hundreds of voices and thoughts. Noah would have yanked the cochlear from his head to stop the roar but he might need to hear instructions from Lieutenant Green. They slipped out a side door of the building. Noah pictured Miguel asking about them when they didn't get on the bus. Sorry that he didn't get to say goodbye.

Corporal Powell was waiting in the car. As soon as she pulled the car into traffic, Noah shouted with his fists in the air, "Woo-hoo! I think we did it."

"Awesome, Noah," said Lena. "I can't believe how you spoke to the Ambassador without my help."

"Me either." Noah leaned into the seat and ran his hands through his hair. "Should I tell you what I heard or wait to tell the captain?"

Lieutenant Green turned in the seat, "Wait. I've let the captain know we are on our way with the intel." He pulled down the visor mirror and smiled at them in the reflection. "You both did a great job. After our meeting with Captain Billings, how about some real New York pizza before we catch our flight home?"

"Sounds great!" Noah said.

Lena nodded beside him.

Noah felt a tingle in his head.

Wish we could tell our parents about it. Lena gave him one of her rare smiles.

Noah signed, "Me too, Lena. Me too."

Chapter 33

"Congratulations!" Captain Billings shook hands with Noah and Lena. "Lieutenant Green said you handled yourselves like pros."

Seeing the captain smile for the first time was strange. He looked like a completely different guy.

Noah leaned forward and asked, "Will it help? You know, what I heard?"

"Absolutely! Based on the information you heard and what we already knew, we have dispatched a team to intercept the truck and rescue the prisoners," said the captain. He signed some papers and handed them to a waiting soldier. "We should be receiving a call any minute updating us on the rescue."

Noah was amazed that the thoughts he heard affected the lives of people so far away. He glanced at Lena and she gave him a thumbs up.

The phone on the captain's desk rang and everyone startled.

"Yes, yes. Good. Good news. Thank you." Captain Billings hung up the receiver and said, "You have served your country well. The rescue was successful, and our people are on their way home to their families."

He stood and motioned for them to the door. "Now, let's get you to the airport so you can go home as well."

Noah turned and hugged Lena before he even thought about it.

She squealed and hugged him back. Then she realized what they were doing.

"Let go of me, you dork!"

But she was smiling. Her thoughts jumped into his. *You did great, Noah.*

"Thanks," he signed.

Lieutenant Green cleared his throat, "I hate to interrupt your celebration, but we need to catch that flight."

He gave a light tug on Lena's braid. "Lena, you go with Corporal Powell to get your gear. You're with me, kid. Everybody, stay sharp."

As they headed to their rooms, the lieutenant said, "Didn't know you were into hugging your partner now."

Noah tried to stay serious but struggled to wipe the smile off his face. "Probably won't happen again."

He felt his face burn.

"I was surprised she didn't slug you!" Lieutenant Green said, then laughed.

"Me too!" Noah said. He watched the lieutenant unlock the door to the room and made a quick safety check. It was good to know someone was looking out for him.

He motioned for Noah to enter.

"Okay, kid," Lieutenant Green said, "I'll get my gear and meet you back here in five. Keep the door locked."

Noah grinned and gave a salute.

The lieutenant clicked his heels and returned the salute. Just before he pulled the door shut he said, "I knew you could do the job."

Noah flipped the lock guard after the door shut. He thought for a minute about all the changes since his cochlear was activated.

Stared at himself in the mirror. He was so relieved the mission was over. That he hadn't messed up. That he wasn't just fooling someone. He wondered what Tod would say if he knew.

A knock came on the door. "That was a fast five minutes," he shouted as he saw the door open and catch on the lock guard.

"Housekeeping," a maid said. "I have towels."

"Oh, sure, come in." Noah pulled back the guard and walked to the side of the bed. He bent down to pick up a pair of socks. Wondered why the maid hadn't waited until they checked out.

He sensed someone standing near him and turned to look. A burning pinch on his neck made him wince. His eyes were open, but darkness was all he saw.

He didn't even know when he hit the floor.

Chapter 34

A mustiness filled Noah's head. So intense it was impossible to pull in a full breath. He forced his eyes open and drowned in darkness. He was certain time had passed but he had no idea how much or where he was. The last thing he remembered was packing to go home. A cough sputtered in his throat and click-squeaked in his cochlear.

"At least I can hear," he said to no one.

"What? Who said that?" a tiny voice rattled somewhere in the dark space.

"It's me. Who are you?" Noah answered.

"Upchuck? Is that you?"

Lena was the only one who called him that. He heard a whimper and then a strange thump-scoot. "Lena? Keep talking so I can find you."

"It's so dark. And that smell," she said.

Noah tried to stand but dropped to his knees when a dizziness made his stomach turn. He crawled toward her voice. His hand touched what he thought was her leg. Something wasn't right.

A dread raced through Noah. "Lena, where's your leg?"

"I don't know! I woke up and...it was gone." A sob exploded from her chest. "Who would take my leg?"

He didn't know which freaked him more, the complete darkness or Lena being out of control. He moved to sit beside her. Stickiness on the wall made him cringe.

"What is the last thing you remember?"

Lena's words were high pitched, like she was trying to hold back tears. "My brain is foggy, but I remember being in the hotel room. Yes. Corporal Powell said to wait in my room while she went to get the car."

"Yeah, I was in my room too." Noah rubbed his forehead. "Lieutenant Green said to wait there while he got his stuff. He said he'd be back in five minutes."

"Someone else was in the room." Noah felt Lena shift her weight. "It was a hotel maid. She said she brought clean towels."

"A maid came in my room, too. She had towels."

Neither one of them spoke for a few seconds.

"Doesn't that seem odd?" Lena asked. "We were checking out. Why would she bring towels?"

"Anything after that?" Noah asked.

"Nothing! Except I think something stung me on the neck."

"Me too!"

"What are the chances bees would get in both our rooms?" Lena asked.

Noah walked his finger to the spot that was still tender on his neck. "I don't think it was a bee, Lena."

"What are we going to do, Noah. I can't think."

Her words sounded muffled like she had covered her face with her hands.

Noah pushed down his own panic. "We've got to stay calm. If we lose it, whoever grabbed us is in complete control."

"I know. You're right, but the smell. It makes me crazy." Lena's breaths were loud, more like gasps. "It smells like the river."

Noah searched his memory. Had he known she didn't like riv-
ers? No, she wasn't afraid of anything. Then he stopped. "Lena, was
that where it happened? Where you lost your leg? Were you in a
river?"

The Lena that Noah had grown to respect and even fear would
have told him it was none of his business. But the Lena next to him
in the dark was broken.

A moan echoed in the dark.

"There was so much blood," she said. "It felt like my leg was on
fire and the blood mixed with the smell of the river."

She stopped and whispered, "I thought I was going to die."

Noah longed for a piece of grape gum to slip into her hand.
But he knew it was going to take more than a few bubbles to calm
her. Without even thinking, he reached for her. She cried into his
shoulder. Cried like no one he had ever heard. If they got out of this
mess, things would never be the same between them. Lena would be
mad, embarrassed that she had let him see her so weak. But, the bond
would be there.

He didn't know how long they stayed like that. A few minutes,
an hour? Long enough for his arm to cramp against the wall. He was
pretty sure she was asleep, so he gently moved his arm and let her
head rest into the corner.

Multi-tone beeping bounced off the walls and a door swung
open. Noah cringed when the bright light blinded him.

"They're awake."

"Good. Bring the boy first."

Noah tensed when he was pulled to his feet by two big-muscled
guys.

"Where are you taking him?" Lena shouted.

Noah tried to fight, but the men held him tight with their solid
arms and vise grip fingers.

"It's okay, Lena," he called to her. "I'll be okay."

The last thing he saw before the men slammed the door shut was Lena trying to stand on her one leg.

She fell with a sickening thud.

The sight burned into Noah's brain until he wanted to hit something. "What kind of a sicko would take her leg? Ugh! Let go of me!"

"Hey, little boy," hot breath hissed near his ear, "you fight, we have ways to keep you quiet."

A bag was pulled over his head causing him to fight for air. More beeping from what Noah thought must be a digital lock on the door trapping Lena. He stopped fighting and forced himself to concentrate.

There was no doubt they had been kidnapped, but by who? He wondered how long they'd been unconscious. Was anyone looking for them? He fought against the panic growing stronger in his chest. Would he ever see his family again? The men stopped dragging him and he heard the same multi-tone beeps. A door squeaked and he was propelled into the air. His shoulder hit something solid and he slid to the floor.

"Ugh," he moaned and ripped the bag from his head.

He heard steps and saw the backs of the two goons exit. More beeps sounded and he was alone.

Like Lena, his brain was foggy, but he remembered two things from camp training.

1. Assess your situation:
   - He and Lena were in trouble.
   - Their only hope might be him.
2. Make a mental note of every detail:
   - Bright white room with one chair and a small metal table.
   - A strong abrasive smell reminded him of Dr. Odor's cologne.

- Concrete walls, tile floor, drop ceiling, a mirror on one wall.
- No windows and cold, so cold.

He was considering standing on the chair to see if he could reach the ceiling tiles when he heard beeps again. The door swung open.

Noah's stomach flipped when he saw the man who entered.

Chapter 35

"Ah, we meet again," said the man from the plane.

"We haven't met," Noah said. "You just followed us."

"So nice of you to notice. Now let's begin." The man turned the chair backwards and straddled it.

The family meeting and Dad sitting that way rushed back at him. Did Captain Billings tell his family he'd been kidnapped or were there more lies? He longed to feel his mom's arms tight around him.

The man clicked some settings on his cell phone and set it on the table. "We know your name is Noah Baker and your little girlfriend is Lena Robertson. We know you have been posing as part of a disabled children's organization but are actually working for your government. That leaves an important question."

He stood and combed his hair in the mirror. "Why would two children be needed by one of the most powerful nations in the world? One that is deaf and the other lame like an injured racehorse."

Noah remained silent. Glad this creep didn't know about the special cochlear. Not yet anyway. He and Lena had to get out of wherever they were before his abilities were discovered. His brain was getting clearer and he knew activating the NT could make an escape happen.

Maybe.

"No answers for me?" said the man. "Let's get you a bit more comfortable."

He stood and motioned for Noah to sit in the chair.

Noah eyes flitted from the chair to the door. He was pretty sure if he refused the chair, the goons would be called to lift him to it. He glanced at the goosebumps on his arms and thought the chair would be better than the cold floor. He groaned as he stood, then dropped his body onto the seat.

"Ah...much better. Is it not?" The man stood directly in Noah's line of vision. "Now, maybe your tongue will be loosened after I tell you we know where your family lives. Your father is at this moment driving his little grass machine in someone else's yard instead of grading the tests from his students. Your brother is running because he made his coach mad at soccer practice."

"Football," Noah mumbled under his breath. "It's called football."

Didn't know why it was important that the name be correct. Maybe because it would be important to Tod.

"Oh, yes. The ball that only one person kicks." The man again combed his mustache in the mirror. "Silly American sport."

He moved to face Noah. "But you haven't let me finish. You might find it interesting that your mother has left work early and is shopping at the mall."

The man was close enough for Noah to smell his breath. "The very one where she bought you those pants."

The man's lips spread into a creepy smile. Must be from a country without dentists. His teeth were crooked and yellow.

Noah looked down at his legs and remembered the black car on their street. The fast trip to the mall to get the required khaki pants. The car stalking them. Speeding off when he confronted them.

"It was you! You were following us. Your window was down and I saw your face before your car almost ran over my foot!"

The man's eyes flitted to the side and he backed from Noah's face. Again, he checked his hair and mustache in the mirror then lit one of his brown cigarettes.

Must have touched a nerve. Maybe the guy got in trouble for being seen by the deaf kid. Noah coughed as smoke from the cigarette reached him. He smiled at the thought of this creep being busted by whoever was in charge.

He needed to distract the man from talking any more about his family.

"Why did you take Lena's leg?"

The man turned. "Ah, the little girl. Even unconscious, so difficult to manage. Much better once we removed the leg."

His heels tapped on the tile floor. "She's the strong one of your team. Is she not?"

Another move in close. Disgusting smile and breath so foul it made Noah's eyes water.

"It is difficult to lead on just one leg."

And then he laughed. He threw back his head.

And.

Laughed.

Noah tasted bile in his throat. Maybe he'd hurl all over the man's precious mustache. The best he could aim for was his shoes. His very expensive looking shoes.

The man jumped back. "You stupid, weak child!"

He pressed a button on the wall.

Noah reached for the NT button while the man was distracted. Just as he dropped his hands from his cochlear, the goons burst through the door. They dragged him from the room. Not even putting the bag on his head.

Noah counted the doors in the hall and the number of turns. A janitor closet door stood open in the last hall before the guards stopped. His brain tingled and thoughts from both guys mixed with the panic of his own. One of the guys started to punch buttons on the wall.

"Wait!" said the other guy. "We forgot the bag."

"Just turn him around."

Noah winced as his arms were pinned behind him and his face pressed to the wall.

"He can't see now." The guy's raw laugh grated through Noah's cochlear.

Noah couldn't see, but the numbers the other guy was thinking came through like a shout.

Eight-five-zero-zero-zero-one.

The door squeaked open and Noah felt his body fly into the room. He skidded across the floor. Landed beside Lena's one foot.

"Hey, you jerks!" she shouted. "Where's my leg?"

Noah smiled, realizing the old Lena was back.

The door slammed shut. But not before Noah saw the pipes snaking across the ceiling. He had an idea.

Lena was still ranting about her leg.

Noah grabbed her arm. "Stop, Lena. Listen!"

He whispered the numbers into her ear in case the dark room was bugged. "Remember those numbers. It's the code for the door."

"Got it!" she whispered back. "Where have you been? What did they do to you?"

"I was in a room down the hall. The guy from the plane and the bench was there. He wanted to know why two kids are working for the government."

Noah decided not to mention the details the man knew about his family. Knew Lena would lose control thinking her family might be in danger. "He made some threats, but then I kinda made him mad."

"What did you do? You didn't tell him did you?" Lena asked.

"No, I threw up. On his shoes." Noah felt his face heat. Waited for Lena's insults.

"Ha!" Lena shouted, then softened her voice. "Way to go, Upchuck. A new defense strategy. Projectile vomit!"

Noah smiled, but knew they had to hurry with a plan to get out of there.

"They'll come for you next." Noah said into her ear. "We're going to be ready when they do. You ever run a three-legged race, Lena?"

Chapter 36

"Can you hear anything, Noah?" Lena asked from her corner.

"Nothing. But the door may be too..." A faint brain tingle caused him to stop.

"Quiet," he whispered. "I need to listen with my head."

That idiot. Always leaves the worst jobs for me.

"Get ready, Lena." Noah jumped to grab where he remembered the pipes were on the ceiling.

He missed the first time. Tried again, caught the pipe with enough grip to swing in the air. The door beeps sounded. The door squeaked open.

Noah swung with all his strength and kicked the guard under the chin.

The man stood frozen, stunned.

Noah swung his legs again. This time aiming for his face. A sickening crack sounded when he made contact with the man's nose. Everything moved in slow motion. And then the man fell face down in a pool of blood from his nose. Noah dropped from the pipe and leaned over the man to check the pulse in his neck. Grateful he'd just been knocked out by the fall. He peeked in the hall. No sign of anyone.

"Help me get his belt."

Lena thump-crawled to help slip the belt from the belly of the unconscious mountain. "I hope this works."

Noah grunted as he shoved the man's legs away from the door enough to let them out, but still propping it open for light.

"Sure, it will. You said you've been in a three-legged race."

"Yes, but I had two legs at the time."

Noah smiled at her sarcastic tone. It made him more confident just hearing her snarky words. "It'll work. Once I get you out of this room and hide you, I'll figure out where we are."

"Sounds like a stupid plan."

"Do you have a better one?" Noah asked as he heaved her up to lean against the wall. "I'll just strap your leg to mine."

He stood close to her short leg and tried not to stare at the stump she'd always been so careful to hide. He wrapped the belt and cinched it tight.

"Here, you hold the long end. That way you'll be able to pull your leg forward with mine."

"Sounds good," she said. "You know I like to be in charge."

Noah laughed and was thankful to see her smile in the faint light.

"Okay, how are we going to do this? I came up with the plan, you make it work."

"Got it!" she said. "On one we use our outside legs. On two the ones strapped together."

"Just think the numbers so no one can hear us," Noah said.

She nodded and her thoughts shouted. *Ready?*

Noah nodded.

One. Two. One. Two.

It worked. Noah slammed the door, locking the guard inside. They made progress, but it worried Noah that they were stopping between every few steps. Someone would come soon to see why the guard hadn't brought Lena to the room for questioning.

"Keep going, Lena. There's a closet just around the corner. You can rest there."

"I don't need to rest. Just go!" Lena said, then panted.

Sweat dripped from her forehead and her face was bright red.

"Sure," Noah replied. "I know. But I can make faster progress once I have you hidden."

He held up his hand. "Look around that corner to see if the hall is clear."

Lena peeked around the edge of the wall. She held up her thumb and they took three more steps to the closet.

When they reached the door, Noah made a silent prayer that it would be unlocked. He twisted the knob and they both slipped through the opening. He found a light switch and flipped it.

Lena unstrapped the belt and hopped to lean against some shelves.

"Sorry it smells like cleaning supplies in here," Noah said.

"Smells like heaven to me."

Noah pressed his lips together. Remembered how broken he'd seen his partner when she told him about losing her leg.

"You can hide behind these boxes while I look for a way out." He helped her hop to the corner and stacked anything he could find in front of her. Tried to make it look normal. "I'm going to lock the door. That might slow someone down if they're looking for you. You can open it from the inside when I come back."

"We'll need a signal, so I'll know it's you," she said.

"Okay. Got any ideas?" Noah asked.

"How about you make gagging noises like you're about to hurl?"

"Very funny," Noah replied. "Let's go with one knock, then two, then three."

"Sounds pretty boring, but I guess it'll work." Lena's crooked smile melted Noah's heart.

"I'll be back as soon as I can." He shut off the light and reached for the handle.

Lena's muffled voice came from behind the boxes. "Hey, Noah."

He heard the shakiness in her words. "What, Lena? I've got to go."

"Don't forget where you put me."

"I won't," he said. He twisted the handle and pushed the lock button.

Closing the closet door, knowing it locked behind him, made his heart beat hard in his chest. He'd promised Lena he'd come back, but what if he couldn't? It didn't help that her thoughts were screaming in his head. He ignored her panic and pressed his back against the wall.

"Why haven't they found the guard?" he whispered to no one.

One, two, three, four halls and he came to a lone elevator. Beside it, stairs led up. None going down.

Above the elevator button, a sign said, *LL – C.*

"Hmm…" Noah said, "If this is C, A and B would be above us and then a ground floor." He walked toward the stair door and started climbing. The next door said, LL-B so he knew he was on to something. His legs ached as he continued up the stairs. When he came to Level 1, he pushed the door open just enough to get a peek.

A large room like a lobby stretched out in front of him. The floor was littered with sawdust and carpenter's equipment. The windows were covered with massive sheets of plastic. No sounds reached his cochlear but the shadows of traffic moved beyond the opaque window coverings. Halfway across the large space was a glass door. Noah took a step to make a run but stopped himself. No way could he leave Lena in that closet.

He pulled the door shut and raced down the stairs. When the stairs stopped, he plowed through the door to the basement. Couldn't wait to tell Lena.

The elevator dinged beside him. He propelled himself behind a nearby couch.

"I'm going to question the girl now," the voice of the mustache man said.

Noah peeked around the couch and saw a woman with red hair talking to the man.

"Is the boat ready?" she asked him.

Their accents sounded similar but not like the Viracochan Ambassador. Noah didn't think they were connected to the mission at all.

"Of course, the boat is ready. We will transport them to the dock right after I finish questioning the girl."

A boat? He and Lena were in even more trouble than Noah thought. There was nothing funny in the situation, but it made him smile when he saw the man's stained shoes.

The woman's cell phone sounded. "I understand."

"What is it?" asked the mustache man.

"We may have a problem. Come with me."

"What about the prisoners?" The man sounded almost disappointed.

"Your questions for the girl will have to wait."

Noah tried to listen to their thoughts, but his panic was so loud in his head, he couldn't sort out their thoughts from his own.

The elevator doors closed behind them. Noah slipped from the couch and slid around corners until he was close to Lena's hiding place. Footsteps pinged through his cochlear. He dropped behind a large laundry cart. Wondered if that's how they'd moved him and Lena from the hotel. The steps echoed off the walls toward the room where they'd left the guard. Noah sprinted for the closet. He struggled to remember the knock code they'd planned. Wished he'd agreed to the gagging idea. One knock, two knocks, three knocks. He waited. Lock beeps sounded down the hall. The closet door opened, and Noah fell in just as a voice shouted.

"They're gone! Find them. Now!"

Chapter 37

"What happened?!" Lena hissed.

Noah ignored her. He pressed the lock on the door and looked for something to brace it. Nothing looked heavy enough.

"They know we escaped." Noah panted and wiped sweat from his eyes. "I heard a lady talking to the man with the mustache. She told him it was time to go."

Noah grabbed Lena's shoulders. "They have a boat and they're taking us with them!"

Lena's thoughts coming through Noah's cochlear were so panicked he reached up to shut off the NT. He couldn't bear to listen.

"What are we going to do?" Lena's lip quivered.

"We're going to get out of here," he said.

"How? I only have one leg, Noah."

Noah stared into her eyes clouded with fear. Lena had always been the strong one. She was the one who pushed to be in charge.

He squatted beside her on the floor. "I've got a plan! Do you trust me?"

"I don't think I have a choice."

Her snarky words made him smile.

"Come on." He grabbed her arm and helped her stand. "We're going to do our three-legged thing again with the belt to the elevator. We're three levels below a deserted lobby with a door to the street."

"Got it!" Lena said. "Is your NT on so I don't have to say anything?"

He reached for the button.

"It's on," he said, and helped her attach the belt to their inside legs again.

He opened the door a crack. "Hall's clear. Let's go."

It took forever to reach the elevator. When running feet echoed through the halls and doors slammed, Lena grabbed Noah and they both dropped behind the couch.

"Forget about those kids. Let's take the doctor and get out of here."

"Yes, sir," said a deep voice.

The sounds grew quiet. Noah whispered into Lena's ear. "Did you hear that? They must have Dr. Odor too. I thought I smelled his cologne."

Noah grabbed the back of the couch and peeked to see if everyone was gone. "Are you okay? You know from when we fell?"

"I'm fine," Lena said. "Let's get out of here before they come back!"

They stood and did their skip steps to the elevator. Noah reached for the button. Lena grabbed his wrist. "Wait! What if someone's on the elevator?"

Noah hadn't thought of that. "We can't climb the stairs like this. I think the elevator is worth the risk."

"Okay." Lena smiled and said, "When did you get so brave, Noah?"

"From watching you! Let's push it together."

They pressed the button and waited.

Noah held his breath. Tried not to second guess his big plan.

The elevator dinged and the doors slid open. Empty. They both blew out their held breath.

"Let's go."

Everything now depended on who was in the lobby.

Noah pushed the L-1 button on the elevator panel. He glanced at Lena as she leaned her head against the wall. They both looked up as the elevator pinged off Level C, Level A. "We're almost there, Lena."

She grabbed his arm. "I'm slowing you down, Noah. Leave me in the elevator and go get help."

Noah pushed down his panic. He wished he could turn back time and tell Captain Billings he didn't want to work for the government. He wished he could run from all of this. All he had wanted was normal.

"Noah? Did you hear me?"

Just as the doors opened on Level 1, Noah unstrapped the belt from their legs. "No way am I going to leave you. We're getting out of this together."

Before Lena could resist, Noah said, "Get on my back, now!"

Lena's eyes grew wide. "No way!" she said.

"There's no time to argue. I'm going to carry you." Noah bent down. "Wrap your arms around my neck."

She was a lot heavier than Noah thought but slowly he hauled her from the elevator and to the front automatic doors. He prayed the doors weren't locked.

He sighed in relief when the door budged open.

People stared at them on the sidewalk in front of the building. Noah had just dropped Lena on a bench when they heard sirens and screeching tires.

Lieutenant Green raced toward them in full military gear. "Get these kids into a vehicle."

"What took you so long?" Noah shouted.

"Good to see you too!" Lieutenant Green grinned. "We've been looking but your trackers didn't show up until a few minutes ago."

"They had us in a basement three levels down," Lena said.

"I guess our GPS trackers couldn't be picked up below ground level. Einstein will need to work on that," said the lieutenant. "Let's get you somewhere safe."

"Those creeps took her leg," Noah said with a sneer. "And they still have Dr. Odor."

A shadow passed over the lieutenant's face. "We'll find your leg."

He didn't say anything about the doctor.

Someone rolled up a wheelchair for Lena and soon they were both in an ambulance with sirens screaming.

Chapter 38

After medical staff checked Noah and Lena, a million questions were asked by a debriefing agent. The missing details of their kidnapping were given to them by Lieutenant Green.

"After I got my gear from my room, I found Noah's door standing open. I called for backup, but you were both gone before we could get to you." He dropped his head, then glanced at the captain. "I'm completely responsible, Captain Billings. I dropped the ball."

"We all dropped the ball," said the captain.

He looked at Noah and Lena. "We won't let that happen again."

"How long were we missing?" asked Noah.

Lieutenant Green said, "Only a few hours. They were able to block most of the hotel cameras. They missed enough for us to find evidence you were carried out in laundry carts."

"That's what I thought," said Noah.

The lieutenant continued. "You were in an abandoned building near the Brooklyn Bridge. Only a mile and a half from the hotel."

Captain Billings interjected, "We're fairly certain this group had no information about your abilities, Noah. Matter of fact, the guard we captured gave us the impression they thought Lena was the main reason you kids are involved."

Noah scooted to the edge of his seat. "The man who questioned me said that, too. That's why they took her leg."

He glanced at Lena. She'd been really quiet since they began the final debriefing.

"You okay, Lena?" he whispered.

She nodded, but Noah wasn't convinced.

He turned toward Lieutenant Green. "I told you he was the same man we saw on the plane, didn't I?"

"Yes, you did." He turned back to the captain. "The guard we captured isn't cooperating as much as we'd like but we'll know more soon. His fingerprints are being run through the database now."

"There's a couple things I need to tell you," Noah said then scrubbed his hands on the legs of his pants. "It may not be that important."

"Every detail is important," said Captain Billings. "These people need to be stopped."

"Well," Noah took a deep breath, "before we started training the first time. You know when we had to give speeches? Anyway, the night before, I noticed a black car on my street that I'd never seen before. When my mom and I went to the mall the car followed us."

Captain Billings turned to one of his aides. "One of ours?"

"Yes, sir."

"That's what I thought, too. I even had my mom stop at a convenience store. The car stopped too and I saw the government guys. They kind of stood out in their black suits. Their car got trapped behind some other cars when we drove onto the street. I thought they caught up with us at the mall parking lot."

Noah stopped to gather his thoughts and rub his sweaty palms. "After Mom stopped the car, I jumped out and ran over to the car."

Captain Billings stood. "That was a very dangerous thing to do!"

"I know. My mom yelled at me about it for the rest of the night. I told her I thought it was someone from school." Noah looked at Lena and said, "But, Captain Billings, the car I ran over to wasn't the government guys I saw in the convenience store. It was the guy from the plane. His window was down as they drove out of the parking lot."

"Lieutenant Green, were you aware of this?"

"No, sir." The lieutenant was on his feet as well.

"I didn't say anything because I just figured it out while that jerk was questioning me." Noah ducked his head.

"Okay, okay," said the captain. "We can't change the past but it is essential that you tell us everything. Even the smallest detail. No secrets. Understand?"

"Yes, sir," whispered Noah, "but I have a question."

"Go ahead," said the captain.

"What about Dr. Odor? What if he tells them about my cochlear and the mind reading thing?"

Noah noticed a strange look between the adults in the room. Wished he could switch on the NT to know why his question made them uncomfortable.

Captain Billings cleared his throat and said, "We searched the lower floors but no sign of him."

Noah's memory flew back to the questioning room. "It's probably nothing, but I thought I smelled Dr. Odor's cologne just before the mustache man came into the room to question me."

Noah scooted to the edge of his chair. "If they talked to him before me, he must not have said anything yet. The man didn't act like he knew anything."

More looks between Captain Billings and Lieutenant Green.

"Good information, Noah. Remember, always tell us anything you notice. Even if it seems unimportant." He stood. "Now, it's time we got you home."

Captain Billings walked to the window and stared at the New York skyline for a few seconds. "You've been through some trauma with these events. Lieutenant Green will be in contact with you about additional debriefing sessions."

The lieutenant handed them cards. "Here is the number you can use to contact me if you need something before that."

He looked at the captain. "Should I tell them the rest or do you want to do it?"

The captain returned to his desk chair. "Proceed, Lieutenant."

The lieutenant sat and rested his elbows on his knees. His hands were clasped in front of him. "Because of the contact you've had with these people, we'll be keeping your tracking devices active. For your protection."

"Do we have a choice?" Lena asked.

Noah knew this would bring her out of her silence.

"Actually no," said Captain Billings. "We'll also keep an eye on your families. Without their knowledge, of course. Like I said, these people are dangerous."

He stood and reached to shake their hands. "We might call you to help us again, if you are willing. No pressure, just something to think about. Your good work helped to avoid our country's involvement in another war. For now, try to lead your normal lives and have some fun. You've earned it."

There didn't seem to be anything else to say. Noah and Lena followed Lieutenant Green from the room.

But Noah wasn't finished. He scratched his ear and clicked the NT button. He knew they were keeping something from them about Dr. Odor.

"Shut it off, Noah," Lieutenant Green said.

Noah glanced at Lena. He pressed the button but not before he heard one thought.

Got to find the doctor before they get any information.

Chapter 39

It was dark when they boarded the flight to go home. Noah wondered what lie had been told to their parents about being later than the original schedule. As they made their way down the aisle to their seats, he looked at each person already seated. Wondered which ones were military. Which could be working for the bad guys.

Lena whispered in his cochlear ear, "You can have the window seat the whole time. You deserve it."

Noah didn't resist and gave her a thumbs up. Didn't mind when he smelled grape as Lena unwrapped the pack of gum Lieutenant Green handed her. He settled into the seat and buckled his seatbelt, excited to see the lights of the city that never sleeps.

It didn't happen.

He fell asleep during the flight attendant's safety instructions.

* * * * * *

In the car after they landed, Lieutenant Green turned to them in the backseat. "You need to do some of your own debriefing before you go to your separate homes. You know, talk things out. You've been through a lot. I think it will help."

Neither Noah nor Lena said anything for a few minutes after the separation window whirred shut. The silence ended when Lena popped three quick bubbles.

"Did Captain Billings actually say to go home and have fun?" she asked.

"It was kind of like he wanted us to pretend it didn't happen." Noah said. "My problem is, how do I act normal?"

Before the mission, after the mission. A new measurement of time.

"I know," said Lena. "I think I'll try out for the track team. Everything is better when I run."

"Good idea," Noah said.

He pictured Lena's braid flying behind her. Smiling like she had the day he saw her on the track.

"I could get the other ear done." He thought of Dr. Odor and wondered if they'd found him yet.

"Your second implant might make you fly like Superman!"

They both laughed but Noah shivered at the idea of letting the government inside his head again.

"Maybe we could talk sometime," said Lena. "I think it would help me. Since we can't tell anyone else about it all."

"That sounds good." Noah hesitated. "But we can't really talk on the phone. I don't trust it. Not even email. You can bet someone's monitoring."

"I guess meeting in the restroom with the water running isn't a good plan."

"Probably not." Noah grinned. "We'll figure out something. You know as friends."

"I guess we are kinda friends now. You know, after you saved my life and all." She smiled and punched him on the shoulder. "The captain did say we should have fun."

She blew another bubble and let it pop.

The car stopped and Noah crawled from the back seat. "Bye, Bubbles."

"Bye, Upchuck."

The car door slammed and Lieutenant Green handed Noah his bag. "You did a great job, Noah. Made me proud."

The lieutenant saluted.

Noah returned the salute and felt his face heat. "Thanks," he said.

Glad the lieutenant couldn't read his thoughts. Glad he didn't know how terrified Noah had been during the whole kidnapping thing.

After the lieutenant crawled back into the car, Noah waved. He couldn't see through the car's dark windows. Was sure Lena was waving too. And then, realizing he couldn't wait another second until he saw his family, he ran up his sidewalk.

The front door flew open. Noah dropped his gear and his mom hugged him like she was never going to let him go.

Dad patted him on the back and asked, "How was New York? The pictures you sent were great, but we want all the details."

"Let him get in the door first," Mom grabbed him tight around his neck and hugged again.

"Owww…" Noah groaned and pulled away. He reached for the spot where the needle had plunged.

Mom stepped back to look at his neck. "What's this?" She touched the raised red place with her cold fingers.

"Oh, I got stung outside the United Nations. Lots of flowers with bees and stuff." Noah hoped that sounded believable. Wondered how many more lies he would need to produce to keep his parents from knowing what he'd been through.

"Did you show Dr. Odor?" she asked.

Noah's stomach twisted at the thought of Dr. Odor and the man with the little mustache.

"No, but Lieutenant Green saw it. He had me put ice on it."

Finally, the truth. They had given both he and Lena ice packs for the puncture wounds.

Noah wondered if Lena was home yet. Knew she was struggling with lying to her parents even more than he was.

"He's fine," Dad said. "I'll get Tod while you get the pizza on the table."

Noah hadn't realized he was hungry until his stomach growled. Remembered the New York style pizza Lieutenant Green promised that didn't happen. The medical people gave him crackers and lemon-lime soda. Probably they wanted to avoid any more stomach issues. He couldn't remember the last time he had real food.

Noah followed Mom into the kitchen and listened to her nervous robotic words while she brought plates and two extra-large pizza boxes to the table. He reached to click on the NT but stopped himself. He was so happy to be home and not on a boat with the mustache man. Happy to know his parents were proud of him.

He was afraid to hear what they really thought.

Chapter 40

N oah lay in the dark, trying to sleep. Trying to shut off the
jumble of thoughts racing in his mind—the mission, the
kidnapping, Lena crying in the musty underground room.
How was he supposed to study about prepositional phrases and cell
mitosis in school while knowing the government was keeping track
of his every move?

He raised on his elbow when the bedroom door opened. Light
fell across his bed from the hall, and Tod's silhouette crossed the room.
It took Noah back to the night before his fake camp. The night Tod's
thoughts revealed he was sure he had killed his little brother in the
car accident. Suddenly all Noah wanted to do was talk to Tod. He
needed to hear what was going on in his brother's head.

Noah reached for his cochlear from the table and snapped it in
place. The sound of Tod's shoe dropping to the floor rushed at him.
He clicked the NT button.

"How was the game on Friday?" That seemed like a safe way to
get his brother talking.

Tod groaned and said, "We lost." His second shoe dropped to
the floor. "But I did make a touchdown."

Noah turned to sit on the side of his bed. "That's great!"

"Yep, it was pretty cool."

Noah felt a brain tingle. *Not as cool as a trip to New York.*

"I'm sorry I wasn't there to see it, Tod. I bet Mom and Dad were excited."

Tod sighed and said, "They were."

Almost as excited as they were to see you.

"New York was really something. Maybe someday Dad will take us there," Noah said. Then he wondered if they would ever be able to go somewhere as a family—if the government would always need to protect them.

Tod huffed and muttered, "Sounds pretty lame to me."

Noah ducked when Tod's shoe came flying across the room.

"Quit talking and go to sleep."

Ah, there it was. Normal life. Just like he had hoped for.